FROZEN
FIRE

FROZEN FIRE

by James Houston

drawings by the author

Aladdin Paperbacks

Aladdin Paperbacks
An imprint of Simon & Schuster
Children's Publishing Division
1230 Avenue of the Americas
New York, NY 10020
Copyright © 1977 by James Houston
All rights reserved including the right of reproduction
in whole or in part in any form.
First Aladdin Paperbacks edition, 1981
Second Aladdin Paperbacks edition, 1992

Printed in the United States of America
10
A hardcover edition of *Frozen Fire* is available from Margaret K. McElderry Books.

Library of Congress Cataloging-in-Publication Data

Houston, James A., 1921–
    Frozen fire : a tale of courage / James Houston; drawings by the author. — 2nd Aladdin Books ed.
        p.   cm.
    Summary: Determined to find his father who has been lost in a storm, a young boy and his Eskimo friend brave wind storms, starvation, wild animals and wild men during their search in the Canadian Arctic.
    ISBN 0-689-71612-5
    [1. Survival—Fiction.   2. Arctic regions—Fiction.]   I. Title.
[PZ7.H819Fr   1992]
[Fic]—dc20
                                                                91-46062

To Eskimo students everywhere and their friends who study in the north or south.

ᔕᐅᕐ

ᐃᓄᐃᑦ ᐊᖃᓱᐃ ᓀᑕᑐᐊᖄ
ᑭᑕᓇᓱᖃᔪ ᐊᖃᔭ
ᓗᖃᓄ ᑭᓗᓇᖃᔪ
ᔕᐅᕐ

Some years ago in the Canadian Arctic a boy was lost. A giant air and land search for him was undertaken. The boy in the face of fearful weather and immense danger showed tremendous courage during his incredible struggle for survival.

This story is based upon many of the true events that occurred during his desperate journey.

James Houston
Frobisher Bay, N.W.T.
1977

FROZEN FIRE

I

MATTHEW MORGAN SHIVERED AS HE STEPPED OUTSIDE
the hotel in downtown Montreal. It was five A.M.,
cold, and black as midnight. He helped his father
and the driver load the taxi, then crawled into the
back seat. Hemmed in by sleeping bags, he watched
the city turn to gray then fade behind them, as the
icy yellow dawn spread through the winter sky.

When they arrived at Dorval Airport, Matthew
struggled out and with his father loaded the baggage cart and pushed it through the swinging doors.
Inside, their heavy Arctic boots squealed on the
polished floor and the sound echoed through the
vastness of the almost empty building. Air India,
Japan Airlines, Eastern Airlines, Air France, Air
Italia, Aeroflot to Russia—all their counters were

vacant at this early hour.

As they rounded the corner, they saw the Nordair agent's desk and a little huddle of people struggling like themselves with Arctic gear. So busy were they all that they scarcely noticed when the frosted east windows touched by the first rays of the early morning sun, flared like gold.

"*Attention! Attention!* Nordair flight number three to Baffin Island is now ready for boarding. *Nordair numero trois est prête maintenant. Montrez vos billets, s'il vous plait!*"

"Hurry! We're late!" his father called to him.

Matthew shivered inwardly with excitement at the thought of flying two thousand miles north into the Canadian Arctic. He remembered again a colored photograph he had once seen of a polar bear crouching over its kill. In his mind's eye he saw the terrifying image of the white bear. It was a frightening vision that had troubled Matthew since the day his father said they would go together to the Arctic. Matthew jumped when he heard his father exclaim.

"Can't be that much!" Mr. Morgan looked and could scarcely believe the weight of their equipment on the scales.

"Put your two bags on gently," said his father. "Our overweight is going to cost a fortune."

Matthew eyed the three big aluminum trunks and waited as the agent, who spoke more French than English, hurriedly tallied up the cost. There was his father's leather suitcase and fat duffle bag and the long metal case that held the transom level, claim stakes and their favorite fishing rods.

"Five hundred and seven pounds," the agent said. "That's . . . let me see . . ." He punched the numbers on the square black computer. "Eight hundred and . . . thirty-one dollars . . . and seventy-five cents."

"Holy smoke! A poor geologist never gets off light." His father groaned. He pulled his wallet out and paid with hundred dollar bills, rubbing each one to see that two were not stuck together. "It's a lucky thing we're going to a place where we won't spend much money, because—"

"I know," said Matthew. "Because we don't have much money."

"Right!" said his father. "You'll see, a helicopter eats money like an elephant eats grass."

Together they passed through security and hurried along the endless corridor until they came to gate sixteen.

The air outside was sharp and cold. They started to mount the makeshift steps leading through the big freight doors into the husky body of the blue and silver Nordair plane. In front of them a nurse was helping a man on crutches.

"Is that an Eskimo?" Matthew whispered, staring at the short, deeply tanned man with wide cheekbones.

"He must be," answered his father. "He's flying with us into Eskimo country."

"I've never seen an Eskimo before," said Matthew.

Hearing the word "Eskimo," the short man paused and, easing his weight, turned and stared at the two Morgans. His dark narrow eyes seemed to search Matthew for every strength and weakness that lay hidden in him.

Matthew was tall like his father, with the same gray watchful eyes, but he had his mother's sandy colored hair. He was slim with narrow hips and a flair to his shoulders that made you know he would be strong. He had been the fastest runner in his school, when he had lived in Arizona.

Matthew was still awkward with his hands, and this was made more obvious because his wrists and ankles had outgrown his clothing. He had hoped his father would buy him two new shirts and a longer pair of pants, but instead for Christmas he had received a pair of steel-toed climbing boots and a book entitled *Geology Made Easy*.

On the first of February his father had told him they were going north together. That meant leaving school within two weeks, but Matthew had moved so many times before that he had made few friends who would miss him in his class.

"This next place will be better," said his father. He had always said that to Matthew and his mother.

The Eskimo just in front of Matthew winced with pain, said "*Nelunuktovingalook*," and started up the aircraft's stairs again.

Three-quarters of the inside of the plane was

loaded with freight lashed into place with strong ropes. Only a dozen seats remained for passengers. There were two Royal Canadian Mounted Policemen, the Eskimo and the nurse, two weather station men with bushy beards and thick green padded parkas, a thin man with steel-framed eyeglasses carrying a leather briefcase stamped *Government of Canada*, and themselves.

The four engines of the sturdy, whale-shaped plane roared into life. It thundered down the airstrip and took off, rising steeply into the clear blue winter sky.

"Welcome aboard Nordair flight three!" said the captain's voice from the flight deck. "Our flying time to Frobisher is estimated to be four hours. The temperature up there is forty degrees below zero Farenheit or minus forty degrees Celsius. That's the one and only time these figures get together."

Matthew looked at his father. He was huge in his bulky eiderdown parka flung open in the heat of the aircraft. He seemed to sit at least six inches taller than anyone else. Matthew's father looked like a football player, with his heavy forehead, his gray, deep-set eyes, his broken nose and his permanently tanned skin that had come from living in the desert and prospecting in the mountains in every kind of weather. Usually Mr. Morgan was in good humor, but sometimes he seemed as restless as a Bengal tiger pacing back and forth inside its cage. His hands were huge and square, and his body was hard as iron from covering miles of ground in search of the valuable minerals that he never seemed to find.

Matthew unzipped his parka.

"Well, Matt, here we go again, flying into a whole new life together," said his father, and he tilted back his seat and stared out the window. Civilization disappeared behind them, replaced by a vast winter forest of evergreen trees and snowy slopes and frozen river courses that spread beneath them.

"I wish Mom was here to see this." Matthew sighed. "She would love—"

"Well, she's not here, and you and I have to get used to the idea that she's not going to be here with us."

Matthew's father turned his face away and looked out the window.

"I know that," said Matthew, "but, I was just wishing."

"Wishing won't change anything." His father drew in a deep breath. "From now on it's just the two of us in this family, and we have to make the best of it. Sometimes, like right now, it's not easy."

It grew hot in the cabin and Matthew fell asleep at the hour when he usually got out of bed. When he woke, his father was talking with one of the Mounted Policemen.

"We'll be there in an hour," said the younger of the two policemen as he moved over and sat beside Matthew. "Look down there. All the trees have disappeared."

Far beneath them Matthew could see an almost endless field of snow broken only by jagged cliffs of rock that cast long blue shadows. Out before them lay the Hudson Straits cracked into an enormous jigsaw puzzle of moving ice, with seawater as black as night glinting between each slowly grinding pan of ice.

"We're leaving the North American continent," said the policeman. "You can hardly tell where the land turns into frozen sea. We're out over Ungava Bay. Across those straits lies Baffin. It's the fifth largest island in the world, part of the Arctic archipelago. You can just see its towering white mountains in the distance. You're the lucky one," he said. Not many kids get the chance to see an island such as that, unless they're Eskimo." He laughed. "I was born in Moose Jaw in Saskatchewan. That's flat prairie country. Now I go out looking for the oceans and the mountains that I read about in school."

"Put on your parkas and fasten your seat belts," said the captain through the intercom. "We're coming in for a landing. It's forty-two below down there, and I have been advised that there may be some ice on the runway."

As they started their descent into the long fiord, Matthew saw the jigsaw pattern of broken ice pans turn into a solid field of snow-covered ice, wind-stripped mountains rising sharply to the east and west.

"That's the Grinnel Glacier," said Matthew's father, pointing. "I've got a feeling right here inside me," he said, patting his chest, "that if I'm ever going to find old lady luck, she'll be hiding right down there. I mean, Matt, I can almost smell the copper. I can see the bright veins glinting in the igneous rock. Down there, somewhere just below us, an Eskimo came into Frobisher last October with some pieces of solid native copper. One of them was so big that he could hardly roll it onto his sled. And you and I, my son, are going to find that whole ore body of critical metal. We'll be rich, I tell you, rich!" He chuckled and slapped his big rough hands together. "After that we'll not turn pale when some airline clerk hands us a thousand dollar charge to pay for freight."

Matthew could remember his mother saying to him, "Your father believes he is always just one step away from some great mineral treasure hidden in the earth. Get used to that idea. He is like a fisherman who thinks a big fish is waiting just beneath the surface for his hook. Who knows, someday he may really find what he is looking for."

There she was, back in his mind again. It was no use. He had no mother now, no house to call his own, only his father and this new place before him half-buried in the snow.

Matthew looked out the window, as they circled. "What are those?" he asked the Mounted Policeman.

"Crashed airplanes—a whole graveyard of them. Lots more are covered up with snow. Look scary, don't they? This airstrip was called Crystal II in the Second World War. Pilots ferrying bombers on the northern route to Europe used to come piling in here in bad weather with almost no fuel left in their tanks, or engine trouble. Mostly they had no choice, poor devils. They landed any way they could."

Matthew heard the plane's engine change their pitch and watched the big wing flaps go down. He gripped the arms of his seat and felt the bump as the squat plane touched the runway heavily and started along the icy airstrip. Suddenly, without warning the big plane lurched and skidded violently sideways, tipping its port wing. Matthew flung his hands in front of him as his whole weight hit the seat belt.

II

THE HEAVY PLANE TEETERED, THEN RIGHTED ITSELF with a shattering scream of tires.

"Phew!" said the young Mounted Policeman, "that was close."

"Sorry about that, folks," said the pilot. "It's that Arctic wind."

The plane wheeled around and rolled slowly in toward the airport tower.

When Matthew with his father and the others stepped outside, their faces were whipped by a stinging blast that came howling out of the north. It seemed to bite the inside of Matthew's nostrils when he breathed, and he quickly pulled the nylon windshield of his parka hood around his cheeks. As the passengers hurried toward the airport building,

Matthew saw swirling spumes of snow blown across the hard-packed drifts along the runway. They rose like golden smoke in the bleary afternoon sun that hung above the western range of mountains.

The airport was small and crowded with people. Most of them were Eskimos. The place was filled with a blue haze, and he could hear Eskimo, English and French, all spoken very rapidly. Everyone wore bulky Arctic clothing flung open, for the air inside was steaming hot. Piles of baggage and strange equipment stood everywhere. There must have been a dozen people who planned to fly south to Montreal on this return flight, and others who had simply come to see their friends depart.

Matthew saw his father's face beam as he greeted the helicopter pilot whom he had known while prospecting south of Ungava Bay.

"Matt, this is Charlie," said his father. "He's the wild Australian I was telling you about. He used to fly over their northern territory from Alice Springs to Borroloola where the desert temperature rises to 150 degrees on a nice warm winter afternoon. Don't ask me how Charlie found his way into Alaska and the Canadian Arctic. Maybe this spring he can teach you how to spot the difference from the air between hematite, that's iron, and common precambrian granite."

"That's a ruddy laugh," said Charlie, as he pumped Matthew's hand. "Your father taught me all the prospecting I'll ever know. I thought pitchblende was a fancy way to throw a cricket ball, until your old man dug up the gooey black stuff and told me how much a ton of it was worth."

"Well, you know plenty now," said Matthew's father. "Matt, you watch him, when you get a chance. He can make his helicopter hover and dance like a big mosquito. I tell you, when we work together, we can almost smell the metal hiding in the rocks."

"That's the truth," said Charlie. "We'd both be rich today, if that slippery mining company hadn't jumped those mineral claims of ours."

"Charlie, you wait and see. It's going to be different this time. Everything's going to be signed on the dotted line and witnessed for us by a dozen sharp-eyed lawyers!"

"I'll believe that when I see it!" Charlie laughed. He was short, with a thick neck and shoulders as wide as a weight lifter. He had fiery red hair and a freckled face. The corners of his mouth turned up in a smile that never seemed to leave him.

"She's right in there, Matt. Matilda, I mean!" Charlie pointed inside the big dark mouth of the hangar. "I try not to leave her out in winter. She hates the cold. It makes her groan and wheeze like a pregnant koala bear."

"Who's Matilda?" asked Matthew. "Your wife?"

"Hell no! She's my new chopper. I call her *Waltzing Matilda*," said Charlie. "A four-seated helicopter. You'll see her. She's a beauty. Painted fancy fire truck red she is. Got all the newest instruments.

They make her smarter than a hawk. She only takes me along so that I can enjoy the ride!"

Matthew laughed. He liked everything about Charlie, as his father said he would.

Matthew turned his head and noticed the Eskimo man on crutches. The nurse, beside him, was looking out the frosted airport windows as if waiting for something or someone. She asked the young Mounted Policeman a question, nodded and went away, apparently to telephone.

A short, plump Eskimo woman had come to meet the man on crutches. She was wearing sealskin boots and a long-tailed canvas-covered parka trimmed with wolfskin. She seemed to be the Eskimo man's wife. A baby on her back stared out at the crowded room. Beside her stood a small girl, a miniature of her mother, and near the man was a boy about Matthew's age, whom Matthew guessed was his son. Here and there in the big room groups of three or four Eskimos sat silently watching everything that was going on. Matthew wondered if he would ever come to know them.

The man on crutches spoke to his son and pointed directly at Matthew. He smiled broadly, showing strong, irregular teeth, and beckoned to Matthew.

Matthew hesitated, then shyly walked toward them.

"*Aiiya!* This my son, Kayak," he said. "Kayak mean small boat. My son, he speak English, he learn in school. You speak to him. *Ataii!*"

"Hello," said the Eskimo boy shyly. "What's your name?"

"Matt-hew Mor-gan," he answered, pronouncing his name with care.

"Where you come from?" Kayak asked him.

"Montreal. But that's not my home."

Fleetingly, Matthew wondered about his home. Was it in Arizona, or British Columbia or Yucatan or Nebraska? He had lived in all those places, yet none of them seemed truly home to him.

"You going to stay and live in Frobisher Bay?" Kayak asked Matthew.

"Yes, for a while, I hope. Anyway, until the summer ends."

"Oh," said the Kayak. "You go to school here?"

"I guess so. What kind of school is there?"

"Round school," said Kayak, holding his hands to form a circle. "Looks like a silver donut. I'll show you, if you want, after I take my father home. The nurse, she's trying to get an ambulance. But my dad says he don't need no ambulance. He wants me to drive him home on his own Ski-doo. You tell her that, will you, after we go? *Ohaneearkeet?*"

Matthew had no time to answer. Kayak's mother smiled at him as the Eskimo family filed out into the freezing air.

Watching them through the window, Matthew saw Kayak and his father sit on the black plastic seat of a battered yellow snowmobile. Kayak roared the engine, and they moved off fast down a narrow snow road. The mother and daughter walked behind. They waved cheerfully at the father and he waved back at them, using his crutches with a wild free movement that made Matthew know just how delighted he was to be home again with his family.

When the nurse returned, Matthew said to her, "The son of that Eskimo man you brought up on the plane asked me to tell you that he would drive his father home."

"Oh," she answered. "Thanks for telling me. I just called the hospital. That man really should have gone there first." She seemed annoyed. "Now I'll never find him up in those little Eskimo houses. He doesn't speak English, you know, and I don't speak Eskimo. But I could tell how anxious he was to get home. It doesn't matter how nice and warm or how good the food is in the hospitals down south. Eskimos only think of getting home. Can you imagine that? I'm always planning ways I can fly south to Florida or the West Indies, with sunshine and palm trees. But Eskimos, they only want to get back to this frozen, windy place. I'll never understand them!"

"Matt, come on now," his father called. "We've got the truck almost loaded."

"Sling those sleeping bags in the back," said Charlie, "and let's go. Matt, you want to jam yourself in between your dad and me, or ride outside?"

"I'll ride inside," said Matthew.

"Wise boy!" Charlie laughed. "It's not far, but the cab of this kangaroo truck of mine even with no heat is warmer than outside."

As they drove past the brightly painted little houses half-buried in the drifts that had been flung up by a giant snowblower, Charlie pointed through the frosted windshield. "Now this is Frobisher. The Eskimos lived here peacefully, they say, for one . . . two . . . three . . . thousand years.

"The poor Eskimos! They've had an awful time of it. Long ago they carefully worked out a way of life as seal hunters and igloo builders in a quiet frozen world."

"Why did they change?" asked Matthew.

"Because suddenly the war came, and we flung a whole new, noisy, crazy world at them, and now we wonder why they have such trouble getting used to it. When this place, Frobisher, was being built, a lot of Eskimos gave up hunting and stopped living off the land and came and helped us win the war at our request. Now the jobs they used to do have mostly vanished. It's the same thing in Alaska, maybe worse." He paused. "We are the ones who helped to cause their troubles. No one knows how it'll end.

"An Eskimo named Simoonee saved my life two years ago."

"How did he save you?" Matthew asked.

"Simoonee used all the old-fashioned Eskimo ways his father and his grandfather had taught him. But that's another story," Charlie said. "See over there? That's the place most Eskimos live. They call it *Ik-hal-oo-weet*. It means 'the fishing place.' The whites here call that hill Apex. It's a lucky thing the Eskimos are strong, tough people," said Charlie. "They were here before us. And if we don't change some of our foolish ways, they may be here long after we are gone."

They stopped in front of a big house. It had been built by the government. It was painted prison gray and had no curtains on the triple-glassed windows.

"I got them to loan you this old house," said Charlie, as he climbed out of the truck. "I don't know what it's like inside. It's been used by anthropologists, mammalogists, ornithologists, climatologists and the Lord alone knows who else. Let's go inside."

They had to throw their weight against the outer door to open it.

"Ruddy great hinges frozen stiff," said Charlie.

Matthew worked hard carrying the bags into the house.

When they were finished, Charlie slammed the inner door and said, "For the Lord sakes! Look at Matty all white around the nose bone. He's gone and let his face get frostbitten. Take off your mitts and hold your warm hands over your sneezer. Don't rub snow on it. That's an old wives' tale that will only make it worse."

Inside were half a dozen army cots.

"Throw your kit on any one of them," said Charlie. He pulled open the kitchen cupboards and looked inside. "You're in luck. The last ones left some bags of tea and . . . instant coffee and . . . powdered milk and . . . sea biscuits and dried beef. So you won't starve. Tomorrow I'll bring you some fresh-frozen Arctic char. They're big, with red bellies," he said, holding out his arms to show their measure. "A kind of salmon-trout we catch up here. The best tasting fish you ever ate in all your life."

Matthew looked at some jars stored in the corner of the cupboard. His nose and cheeks burned like fire as the frost let go its grip.

"Don't touch those bottles," Charlie warned. "It's formaldehyde for preserving polar bear livers. Did you know that a polar bear's liver is about the only thing in the Arctic you cannot eat? It's so rich in vitamin E that it could kill you. That's true. Even a husky dog will die from it."

"Are there many polar bears around here?" Matthew asked.

"Not many right here because they hate the sound of engines. But down the bay there's lots of them. When I fly over, I often see them hunting for seals out there on the moving ice."

For a second time that day Matthew had a frightening photographic vision of the great white bear.

"This house will be fine for us," his father said. "If you come back tonight, Charlie, I'll get my maps out, and we can plan our attack on the newest, biggest copper mine in North America!"

"Sounds great to me," said Charlie. "But relax, you two. I'll come tomorrow. We don't do things quite as quick up here as they do in Melbourne or Toronto or New York, remember?"

"That's right," said Matthew's father. "It's *mañana,* as the Mexicans say. Tomorrow will have to do, I guess. But remember, I'm nearly out of money, and our careful planning is the only thing that is going to save me at the bank. I haven't forgotten what a day's flying in that whirly-bird of yours can cost me."

"Speaking of cost," said Charlie, "I ruddy near forgot the most important thing."

He ran out to his truck and hurried back again.

"Here they are," he said, handing Matthew's father a big mailing tube. "Judging by the label and the insurance, they're the new color aerial photographs you ordered. They're awfully expensive compared to the old survey maps."

"They sure are," said his father, looking at the invoice, "but I think they're going to be worth it."

"Pip, pip," said Charlie, and he made the frozen hinges squeal like little pigs as he slammed the door behind him.

"It's cold in here." Matt's father shivered. "Keep your parka on until I light the stove. What would you like for dinner? Oatmeal porridge or a pair of nice hard pilot biscuits soaked in tea?"

"I'll toast mine," said Matthew, and he purposely burned them black on both sides.

"I don't know how you stand that charcoal," said his father.

'You chose the main course." Matthew laughed. "I'll make dessert."

Taking out his sheath knife, he cut a chocolate bar in half.

When they had finished eating, Matthew's father slapped the table with his massive hand. "This is the place, Matt. Up here a man can call his soul his own." He pulled off his boots, pants and sweater. The camp cot groaned as he burrowed down into his sleeping bag. "Just the two of us, enough to eat, and a good warm place to sleep. What else could anyone want . . . except maybe about five million pounds of pure red copper at the current market prices! Then maybe we'd go hunting diamonds in southern Africa or emeralds up the Amazon or rubies in Sumatra."

He laughed and looked at Matt. "This trip should turn you into a really sharp geologist. Study that book I gave you. Books can teach you almost everything, except the thrill of finding metal hidden in the earth."

Matthew sighed. "If I stop going to school and read that book, do you think I can just go out with you and learn to recognize the minerals?"

"No," said his father. "You need to go to school, for a whole lot of different reasons."

"Another place, another school." Matthew sighed and relaxed. The soft warmth of the sleeping bag surrounded him and he fell asleep.

At dawn Matthew woke and watched his father's breath rising like kettle steam. He thought, my dad sounds hard and tough sometimes, and he is tough, always going someplace wild where life is hard. He loves frozen places and boiling hot deserts where there are no trees or overburden to cover up the geological formations. If he was gentle and liked to sit placidly in front of fireplaces or on beaches under palm trees, he would be a different person, he would never live this kind of life. I'm glad he brought me with him, even into this cold place. I like him just the way Mom liked him. I like him just the way he is.

His father rolled over and shouted, "It's bitter cold in here! Matt, how would you like to practice lighting that propane stove?"

"I could learn later," Matthew answered.

"Come on, lazy bones, I'll show you," said his father. "I'm a teacher." He leaped out of his sleeping bag, his woolen long johns still newly white like a TV advertisement.

Matthew crawled out of his sleeping bag, stepped into his boots and parka and crouched, shivering, beside his father.

"First you light the match and hold it close to the burner, then turn the stove on very . . . s-l-o-w-l-y."

Matthew watched a blue flame spread around the ring.

"Now," said his father, "I've done my part. You get some water for the coffee."

"The taps don't work," said Matthew.

"Of course not—and there's no flush toilet either. Everything's frozen tight. That's why we don't pay any rent for this old dead heap of a house. Charlie says the ice is piled outside the back door. So out you go and get it. Lots of luck!"

"Why don't we use snow?" asked Matthew.

"Because," his father answered, "dry snow burns black in a pot, if you're not careful. And, even if you manage not to burn it, you have to fill it with snow three or four times to get one pot of water. Ice melts into almost the same volume of water. Lesson ended, demonstration beginning. Go and get some ice quick!"

Matthew fought with the back door until it opened with a jerk, then climbed over a five-foot snowdrift that was hard as concrete. He saw ice blocks piled on a wooden platform with a thin steel ice pick stuck in one, upright like a dagger. Awkwardly he chipped ice into the big aluminum kettle, as he felt the intense cold grip him through his parka and his underwear.

He jumped back over the snowdrift, slammed the back door shut, ran through the house, plunked the kettle on top of the burner and leaped back into his sleeping bag.

"That's the last time I go outdoors without my pants," howled Matthew.

"Now you know you're not living in Arizona!" His father laughed, as he shook some oatmeal into the pot.

"Phew," said Mr. Morgan, when Matthew started

cooking. "The smell of that biscuit burning reminds me of your mother. She used to burn the toast. Remember?"

Matthew did not answer.

"That can't be the school," said Matthew. "It looks more like a round silver spaceship with red markings."

"Charlie assures me it's the school, even if it's got no windows showing. Come on. Let's go inside," said Matthew's father.

In the principal's office his father shook hands and said, "What does one have to do here to enroll his thirteen-year-old son in midterm?"

"Just supply the boy," answered the principal with a smile. "We're used to families coming and going. Your name is . . . ?"

"Matthew Morgan. I was in grade eight in Arizona."

"Well," said the principal, who wore a heavy turtleneck sweater and had a bushy beard, "you can try that same grade here and see how it fits! I know they have a spare desk for you."

"Thank you," said Mr. Morgan. "Then I'll just leave Matt here with you. I have some work to do. Matt, I guess you know the way back . . . home, I mean . . . to the big gray house."

"Yes," said Matthew, as his father disappeared.

The principal introduced Matthew to his new

teacher. The classroom was not so different from others he had known except that the light came from the ceiling's fluorescent tubes to offset the winter's darkness. He counted twenty-six other students; eighteen of them, he guessed, were Eskimos, the others mostly Canadians from the south.

"This is Matthew Morgan," said the teacher welcoming him. "He's from Arizona—"

"And British Columbia," said Matthew proudly, "and before that Mexico."

"I'm from British Columbia," said a tall thin girl. "Vancouver. Where are you from?"

"The Kootanys," answered Matthew.

"I bet your dad's a miner," said the girl.

"A geologist," said Matthew, "and he teaches geology sometimes when he's not prospecting."

"Who knows what a geologist does?" asked the teacher.

"Studies people," guessed an Eskimo boy.

"No," said the teacher, "rocks. Matthew's father studies minerals and rock formations. Anthropologists and sociologists study people."

"Hello." Matthew heard a voice whisper behind him and, turning, recognized Kayak, the Eskimo boy from the airport, the one whose father had been on crutches.

"You remember me? I'm Kayak."

"Sure, I remember you," said Matthew. "Was that your snowmobile?"

"No," said Kayak, looking disappointed. "It belongs to my father. But maybe I'll have one next year. See you after school."

The class was studying geography, but as the morning went on Matthew saw that Kayak was working in another way.

"What's that you're making?" whispered Matthew, seeing that Kayak was bending over his desk, his right hand moving in short, secretive strokes.

"Oh, this," he said, looking up to make sure the teacher was not watching, "this is going to be a *nanungwak*, a small likeness of a polar bear." He held it up so only Matthew could see. "I'm carving it out of a bear's tooth. Then I'm going to hang it around my neck. It's going to bring me very good luck."

"Here comes the teacher," Matthew whispered.

"That's bad luck," said Kayak, and he slipped the short file, the steel wool and the half-carved bear's tooth into his shirt pocket.

"What is the capital of Afghanistan?" the teacher asked, pointing her finger straight at Kayak.

"*Kowyeemungilunga*. I don't know," said Kayak.

"Well, if you would do more studying and less carving, you would know. How do you expect to earn a living?"

"By hunting and carving," answered Kayak. "That's the way my father earns his living. He can't even say 'af-gun-ee-stan.'"

The teacher shook her head. She walked back to

her desk. "Matthew, what rare mineral is found in Afghanistan?"

"Lapis lazuli," said Matthew. "It's peacock blue in color. It's a semi-precious stone."

"Listen to that." The teacher laughed, pointing to Kayak. "Matthew knows about Afghanistan and all its minerals. He's going to be a geologist one day just like his father."

"That's good," said Kayak. "He goes to Afgunee-stan and hunt blue stones, I stay here and hunt caribou and carve just like my father. That way Matthew and me we both have work."

It was dark at four o'clock when Kayak walked back to the big gray house with Matthew. He wore only a purple windbreaker, thin blue jeans, and a multi-colored woven hat. He moved easily along the snowy road. With his hands shoved deep in his pockets, he didn't seem to care about the cold.

"What's over there?" asked Matthew, pointing toward the mountain range across the frozen bay.

"Nothing," said Kayak. "Nothing at all, except some wolves and foxes. Oh, maybe you mean King-merok? It's about one hundred and fifty miles that way and south. I got a very nice aunt and uncle living over there. And the girl I'm going to marry. She lives over there. I only saw her once when I was little."

"My gosh, you seem awfully young to think of getting married!" Matthew exclaimed.

"Well, she was promised for me by her father and my father when she was just a baby in her mother's hood."

"And you've seen her only once?"

"Yes, once," said Kayak. "She is shy the way girls ought to be and she smiles nice. She's going to be a real good sewer because her mother's teaching her."

"A wife!" said Matthew. "I've never even thought about a wife."

"I know some girls around here would make you a lovely wife," said Kayak, "if they're not already spoken for."

At the door Kayak said to Matthew, "I got to go now," and, turning, ran along the snow-filled road.

Inside Charlie was sitting on Matthew's bed and his father had maps spread out, covering half the floor.

"Look at this," Matthew's father called to him. "This is only one of those pieces of heavy metal that the Eskimo found and brought into Frobisher last fall before the snow covered everything. Take a good look at it, my son."

With a knife Matthew's father made a bright scratch across its surface. "Ninety-seven percent pure copper. Just imagine when we find the rest of the deposit! We will hire you and your Eskimo friends to help us stake the claim."

In a quieter voice, his father asked. "How did it go at school today?"

"Oh, it's about the same as all the others," Matthew answered.

"That's fine," Ross Morgan said, but he was thinking of copper fortunes, not of schools.

"So, Charlie, you agree we'll start out by flying over here?" He pointed at the map.

"Righto! That looks good to me," said Charlie. "The wind and sun have lifted most of the snow off the south face of the mountain. We may see something over there."

Mr. Morgan took a red wax pencil and marked a square on the map between his feet. "How soon can we get started?" he asked, and Matthew could hear the familiar hurry in his voice.

"I got some engine parts being flown in tomorrow and, if I'm lucky, I can have them in place next day. We could go then, but the weather station says there's a big storm system moving over the Greenland ice cap, pushing west. That could hold us up."

"Well, you get the parts in and the helicopter ready. Lots of times these storms the weather people talk about blow out to sea."

"That's sometimes true," said Charlie. "I'll get Matilda ready and after that we just have to wait and see what happens. So, Matthew, how's it feel you being back in school?" asked Charlie. "You got any pretty girls in your class?"

"Some," said Matthew, "and I've got a friend named Kayak. He walked home with me. Do you remember him? His father was on crutches in the airport."

"Sure," Charlie answered. "I know that boy, Kayak. I like him and all his family. They're good people."

"Kayak told me his father broke his leg when he was hunting. He was driving his snowmobile through rough ice and got his leg caught between a frozen hummock and the machine. Kayak's father says that machines are not so good for hunting. He likes dog teams unless you're hunting every day for food."

"His father's right," said Mr. Morgan. "Things are changing everywhere. I'm glad you're making friends. Charlie and I will fly away for a day or so, but you'll be fine here, won't you? You know how to get the ice and light the stove. I'll buy some tins of food for you. You won't mind staying alone?"

"No," said Matthew. "I'll be all right by myself."

The next day Matthew ate his lunch at school with all the other students.

"What's it like? At school in Ari-zoona?" Kayak asked him.

"Oh, not so different, except that it's boiling hot outside instead of freezing cold. Right now the cactus must be blooming, that's the nicest time of year."

When the last class of the day had ended, Matthew gathered up his books and stamped into his heavy boots and pulled on his parka. It was growing dark outside.

"You want to come home with me to my house?" Kayak asked. "I'll show you something good made by my dad."

"Sure," said Matthew. "Where do you live?"

"Up in the Eskimo town. The *kalunas* call it Apex. We'll hitchhike a ride up there."

"*Kalunas?*" said Matthew.

"*Ayii, Kalunas.* That's the Eskimo way to say white people. It means you've got bushy eyebrows. Well, you haven't got bushy eyebrows, but it was the thing my people, the *Inuits*, noticed most about the white whale hunters who first came here. They had long hairy eyebrows. My grandmother told me those old whalemen were lovely dancers and they used to give parties on board their ships and give away good presents and play their accordions all night long."

The first truck that passed them that afternoon was a snowblower. The Eskimo driver waved at Kayak.

"That's my sister's husband. He's from Pangnirtung. He works for the government, makes lots of money."

Matthew stuck out his thumb as the next car passed.

"Oh, don't do that to them," said Kayak. "They're the Mounted Police. They don't like kids hitchhiking."

A pair of snowmobiles came racing up the road. Kayak ran out and danced a jig in front of them. They stopped.

"My cousins," he yelled at Matthew. "You get on with Namoni. I go with Ashoona. I bet twenty-five cents we beat you to my house. Come on, we'll race you."

III

NAMONI SMILED AT MATTHEW AND POINTED TO THE black plastic seat behind him. Matthew jumped on and the two snowmobiles raced three miles up the road at breakneck speed, swerved through the tiny village and slithered to a stop in front of Kayak's house. Namoni and Matthew won by half a second.

"I owe you twenty-five cents," said Kayak. "My cousin Ashoona says he's got dirty spark plugs. *Nakoamiasit!*" he shouted to both drivers. "That means 'Thanks a lot' in Eskimo. You got to learn to speak *Inuktitut* if you going to live up here."

"I'll try to learn," said Matthew.

"We don't say Math-you hard like white people do. We say Mattoosie—like singing. We make your name sound smooth as snowbird feathers."

Kayak's family house was small, like a plywood shoebox half-buried in the hard drifts of snow. It was painted Chinese red and bright lime green. The battered yellow snowmobile was standing out in front. A faint light shone through one frosted window.

"What's that up on the roof?" asked Matthew.

"Oh, those are seals," Kayak explained. "My father, Tugak, got them out there on the ice. My dad's a famous shot," he said, pointing an imaginary rifle toward the sea ice. "He's teaching me. We go out every weekend and on all school holidays. And those are the back halves of two caribou we got. We keep them on the roof so my dog won't eat them. He's a big husky and he loves meat!"

They ducked through a low entrance made of hard snow blocks and entered a dark winter porch that smelled of rancid seal fat. Kayak pushed open the door and walked in. Matthew followed him.

Only one kerosene lantern lit the house. It sat in the middle of the floor. There were no chairs in the room, only a low handmade table covered with scattered plates and half-empty tins of food, and a number of beds covered with a tumble of blankets, clothing and caribou skins. It was very hot inside the house.

Kayak got a thick china mug and poured something black out of the kettle on a tiny stove.

"You want a cup of tea? Sit over there," he said, moving a sleeping child to one side.

"Oh, I'm all right," said Matthew. "I'll just stand."

He blinked his eyes, adjusting to the darkness, and the single pool of light. He saw a woman looking at him. She was sewing, sitting on the floor.

"This is my *anana,* my mother. Her name is Elizabee. You know, her name is like Her Majesty, the Queen Elizabee of England. That's where she gets her English name."

"Hello," said Matthew. "I'm glad to meet you."

"*Kenokiak? Shogishapik?*"

"My mom doesn't speak any English," said Kayak. "She asks me who you are." He answered his mother, "*Iluajuk.* I just told her you're my good friend. Sort of like a relative of mine."

Kayak's mother smiled warmly, showing all her square white teeth. She pointed at a cardboard box.

"She offers you a nice store biscuit," Kayak said. "Mattoosie, you take the biscuit from my mother. Not nice to refuse food, first time in somebody's house."

They heard a grunting from another bed and Kayak's father sat up, holding his leg out stiffly before him.

"I got to help my dad outside. He wants to let out water."

When they came inside again Kayak helped his father back onto his bed. "He says he thinks there is going to be a storm with lots of wind."

Matthew heard a sort of moaning and saw a small man lying on a bed. He had an accordion resting on his chest.

"That's my uncle Parr," said Kayak. "Sometimes he feels bad."

Matthew saw a match strike in the darkest corner of the room and watched an old gray-haired woman bend forward and light something. It was a stone lamp of a kind new to him. It was two feet long and oval in shape, with a pool of something liquid shining in it. She carefully tended the wick with the handle of a teaspoon.

"That's my grannie over there. She's *Annanachiak*. She's lighting her seal oil lamp so you can see my father's carving."

Tugak reached down and pulled away his polishing cloth. There on the floor was a bear as long as Matthew's forearm. It seemed to move in the flickering light as though it were a living thing. Its head thrust forward, its legs spread out in a rolling running motion.

"Oh," said Matthew, for he had never seen anything like it.

"My dad carved it out of an old piece of whale bone he found down on the beach."

Kayak's father spoke to him in Eskimo. "He says maybe my great-grandfather killed that whale a long time ago. Now he says he uses the bone to bring him luck. Look, the bear's teeth are made with ivory. Don't touch them. They are sharp," Kayak said.

The old woman said something to Kayak in a high shaky voice.

"My grannie says to tell you she lived almost all

her life at Akeeaktolaolavik, in an igloo in winters, and summers in a sealskin tent. She only came here, she says, when my grandfather was getting old and sick. She can't go to sleep nights without the light of her lamp. She's kind of scared of the dark. She says there's lots of strange things like ghosts and spirits roaming around in the dark. Do you believe that?"

"No," said Matthew. "But don't tell her I said that."

"Don't be afraid to talk. Say anything you want. I'm the only one in this house speaks English, except my sister Pia, and she's away."

The old grandmother spoke to Kayak in a gentle voice. Kayak listened carefully.

"She wants me to tell you that when she first saw you, she thought you were a young white polar bear. She says it was no dream, but now you look ordinary to her, like all the other *kalunas*. Except, she says, you got a nicer smile."

"Where is your grandfather," Matthew asked him, peering into the dark corners of the room.

"He's lying up there in the graveyard behind this house. He told me lots of things before they took him there and they piled the stones on top of him."

Suddenly the door was flung open and a man came in shouting and singing in Eskimo, noisily stamping the snow off his boots.

Kayak's mother rose quickly from the floor and went and sat on the bed beside her husband. The man held out his hand to Kayak's father.

"That's another uncle of mine," Kayak said. "He's drunk again. And he wants my father to give him money to buy more *imialook*—that's what *Inuit* call whiskey."

Kayak's father said something, and his uncle kicked over the lantern. Before it could set the place on fire, Kayak quickly stamped out the flames. The old grandmother pointed her finger at the man and screamed something. Kayak's uncle paused, weaving back and forth. Grunting, he lit a cigarette then turned and staggered out the door.

Kayak shook his head. "I don't know what makes him like that. When I was little, out at camp, he used to be the best hunter, best dog-team driver in this whole country. Now he lives here. He doesn't do anything. He's got no dogs, no rifle. He's just sad in the daytime and gets drunk when night comes. Says he wants to go back out on the land and camp, but he's got nobody to go with him. He says the whites don't like him, nobody likes him. That's what he says. I don't know what is going to happen to my uncle."

Matthew finished the tea and biscuit and said, "I better go back to our house now, or my dad will wonder what's happened to me."

"Sure," said Kayak, and he picked up a battered alarm clock and looked at it. "It's easy to get a ride. Lots of Eskimos have to go to the hospital tonight for X-ray. My grannie's supposed to go, but she won't go. She says God and the little spirits already know the day her soul is going to leave her body. Doesn't need some young man or girl in a white coat to look inside her body with a magic box to tell her that.

"It's OK now," he said, peeking out the door. "My uncle's gone away."

Matthew had only been outside the little house for a minute when a snowmobile raced past him, turned a tight circle on the side of the road and came back to pick him up. It was an Eskimo who gave him a fast ride down the long white snow road that curved toward the government house.

"Thank you for the lift. *Nak-o-mik*," he shouted, using his first Eskimo word meaning thank you.

The Eskimo waved at him as he ran inside their big gray house.

"I was up at Kayak's place," said Matthew to his father.

Mr. Morgan did not look up from his maps, but he muttered a greeting. He had his protractor in his hand and was measuring the scale of miles. In the corner by the door Matthew saw his father's canvas backpack ready, with the bag of claim stakes, his ice axe, and his steel-pointed rock hammer.

"Did you notice if the stars were out?" he asked his son.

"Yes, some," answered Matthew. "But it's hazy and they're hard to see. There's more wind now."

His father went outside and searched the sky. "It's not too bad. Still some stars in the west," he said, "and that wind should die by morning."

"Kayak's father says he thinks there's going to be a storm."

"Well, Eskimos can be wrong like everybody else. Charlie's working on the helicopter. She'll be ready to go in the morning. We'll leave as soon as there's any light.

"Now, Matt, I want to tell you something important before I go—something I haven't told Charlie or anybody else. I don't think this piece of native copper originally came from anywhere near where that Eskimo found it."

"How do you know that?" asked Matthew.

"Well," said his father, "the study of geology is a lot like detective's work. First of all, look at this piece of copper. Tell me what you see."

"Well, it's so heavy I can hardly lift it," said Matthew, "and you have been cutting at it with an axe and scratching it."

"Wrong. No human did that heavy cutting," said his father.

"Who did?" asked Matthew.

"I think nature made those deep cuts thousands of years ago. Look here at these big aerial photographs of the other side of Frobisher Bay. They were taken in August, when there was almost no snow covering the ground."

Matthew nodded.

"Now, what do you see that's strange in those colored aerial photographs?" his father asked him.

"Well," said Matthew, "I see some long scratches running this way."

"No," his father said. "You've got it backwards. They're running that way—southeast."

"How do you know that?" asked Matthew.

"Because we know that thousands of years ago the glacier was moving slowly in that direction, and that glacial ice was carrying this piece of copper and it dragged it over the old surface rock, grinding it, scratching it."

"Maybe just any old stones made those marks."

"No, not just any old stones." He handed Matthew his big magnifying glass. "Look there, beyond the shadow of that gully, and tell me what you see."

Matthew studied the photo carefully. "Well, I can't see anything except that most scratches in other places are white or gray, and lots of these scratches are blue and green."

"Right," said his father. "You've got it! Copper when it's weathered turns blue-green."

"You mean that's copper—there?" He pointed at the photograph.

"No, it's not. It's just the thin marks and traces that the copper left behind, like a pencil lead dragged over a piece of paper thousands of years ago. Now look up here. More green scratches. And here," said his father, pointing further up the map. "Now look way up here."

"I can't see color any more. Just the white and gray scratches."

"Exactly," said his father. "So what does that mean?"

"That the copper wasn't up there?"

"Good thinking," said his father. "I think the glacier turned that copper up right here and dragged it south with some other pieces and dropped it when the glacier melted. It's called copper float. Look there. That's exactly where the green lines start, at the southern base of that big cliff. I think we are looking at what miners call 'the mother lode'! There must be a huge deposit of copper right there." He pointed at the map. "The thing I've looked for half my life!"

"Holy smoke!" exclaimed Matthew, using a favorite expression of his father. "You *are* a good detective. What does Charlie think of this?"

"Shhh," said his father and glanced toward the closed door. "I told you—Charlie doesn't know about this—no one does, and I'm not going to tell Charlie till we're flying in the air."

"Why?" asked Matthew.

"Well," said his father, "Charlie has a habit of partying with his friends most evenings. And when his good-natured Australian tongue starts wagging, you never know what secrets he might tell."

Matthew took up the magnifying glass and studied

the green scratches again. "Too bad," he said, "you'll never see them on the rocks out there this time of year because they'll be completely covered with snow. You'll probably have to wait until summer."

"I'm not waiting until summer," Matthew's father growled. "I've been caught asleep before and lost a fortune. Waiting is why we're poor today! These new color photo maps were issued by the Canadian topographical survey less than three weeks ago. And by now lots of geologists, prospectors and mining companies will have had a chance to study them. I'm not the only one who could guess the meaning of those blue-green lines.

"Remember, Matt," said his father, "it feels like winter out there, but it is March already. And if you look at the south side of the hills, you can see a lot of rocks exposed by the spring sun. I believe the south face of that cliff has seen enough good weather for me to gather mineral samples. And if they look right, we'll come back here and get you and a half-dozen Eskimos to help us, and together we will stake our claims before anyone's the wiser. Imagine, Matt, that copper deposit has been cooked and bubbled up by the earth's inner fires and has waited millions of years for me and this fancy colored photograph to get together. I tell you, Matt, I've found it. At last, I've found it! This time we'll strike it. We'll be richer than a pair of kings!"

He flung the map roll in the air and danced around

the room. The whole house seemed to tremble from his powerful weight.

The door swung open and Charlie stepped inside. "What's all the dancing for?" he asked.

"Oh, Matt and I are just having a little celebration of our own. We're glad to be up here together."

"Well, you wouldn't be dancing like a jolly swagman if you'd seen this weather chart." Charlie snorted. "They say a nasty storm system is moving in over us. Nordair says their scheduled flight may be delayed. They asked me if you know the group of mining men who are planning to come in tomorrow. Are they friends of yours?"

"No, they're not. Who are they? What are their names?" asked Matthew's father, looking worried.

"I don't know," said Charlie. "But they have asked to hire me and the Matilda and they have over a ton of prospecting equipment with them on the Nordair flight. They must be rich!"

Matthew's father frowned, then looked Charlie straight in the eye, spread his hands and said, "See what I mean, Matt? We've got competition." Then turning, he growled, "Forget them Charlie. I'm all packed. Let's go look at the great outdoors!"

Matthew watched them standing in the snowy road, looking anxiously up toward the sky.

"It looks pretty good to me," his father said as they came back through the door. "I tell you what let's do. We'll go out in the morning soon as it's light, have a look along the edge of the Grinnel Glacier, and then get back here before dark, before that storm comes in."

"It's your money, Ross Morgan," Charlie answered. "You can do with it as you please. As long as I can see a few hundred yards, I'll fly the Matilda anywhere. But I'm telling you I would wait until this storm system clears out of this part of the country."

"Charlie, I want to try it in the morning," Matthew's father said determinedly. "Let's meet at six A.M."

"You're the boss," said Charlie. "I'll file my flight plan with the tower at the airport tonight, so we won't waste time tomorrow. It's the east end of the Grinnel Glacier, is it?"

"Yes," said Matthew's father, and he hesitated. "Yes. That's where we're going."

"What did he mean 'file a flight plan'?" asked Matthew after Charlie slammed the door.

"Well, he's going to tell the tower where we're flying just in case—well, just in case of emergency."

"But you're not going there tomorrow. That's southwest of here. You're heading north."

"Didn't you hear him say there's prospectors coming in here? You can bet your boots they've been looking at those new aerial maps. I'm not going to draw them a treasure map and leave it over at that tower! Would you? The first thing they'll ask tomorrow is, 'Where did Ross Morgan fly today?' And the tower will be glad to tell them if they really know.

See what I mean, Matt? You're the only living soul who knows what I know. And if anyone asks you before we get back, you keep your mouth clamped shut. You hear me?"

IV

MATTHEW WOKE WHEN HE HEARD HIS FATHER DRESS-
ing in the darkness. He rolled over in his sleeping
bag.

"No need for you to get up, son. It's only five-thirty
and I'm going to get a little exercise walking down
to the hangar."

Matthew saw him sling his backpack on and pick
up the rest of his gear.

"Aren't you going to have some breakfast?" Matthew asked.

"No," said his father. "You know—my stomach's
always just a wee bit jumpy when I feel excited. And,
Matt, I'm excited now—because I feel lucky—something's going to happen to me, to us."

"Good luck, Dad. Is the weather good outside?"

"I don't know. I'm afraid to look. Anyway, we'll be back just at dark. You make yourself some breakfast and you'll have your lunch at school. Good-bye, Matt."

"Good-bye, Dad."

The door closed and Matthew could hear the snow beneath his father's boots squeal in the bitter cold. Matthew waited, listening to the big house creak in the Arctic silence. He thought of his mother. He had never felt more lonely in his life.

He must have slept again, for when he awoke, weak morning light filled the room and he was afraid he'd be late for school. He jumped up, flung on his clothes, grabbed a hard ship's biscuit, burned it black on both sides and gnawed it as he hurried toward the new school building.

The wind was blowing down the winter road, kicking up a thousand snow devils, causing them to whirl in icy smokelike patterns. The sky in the east was heavy gray and Matthew could hear a ghostly moaning high above him.

They'll be back in six or seven hours, he told himself. They'll beat the storm.

By noon it had grown almost as dark as night and when Matthew looked out the school door, he could not even see the road.

"That's a big storm coming out of the mountains," said Kayak. "Did your dad and Charlie fly this morning?"

"Yes," said Matthew, "but I guess they turned

around. They must be back by now."

"I hope so," Kayak said. "It's going to blow a lot out there. No good for animals or hunters. Everybody hates a wind like that."

When school let out, Matthew said he was going to walk home.

"Oh no, you're not," said Kayak. "A radio man tried to walk only a little way last spring in a storm like that. They found him frozen dead, sitting stiff as stone in a snowdrift by the road. We go in the school bus now."

The school bus stopped before the big gray house and the Eskimo driver opened the door for Matthew to get out.

"You all right by yourself in there?" asked Kayak.

"Oh sure! My dad's inside by now, or if he's not, he'll be here soon."

"I don't know," said Kayak. "I listened all morning to hear them. Nothing sounding. Now it's too bad for any kind of airplane to fly."

Matthew had to fight against the force of the wind to make his way—a dozen steps between the bus and the house. He could scarcely see the door, for he was almost blinded by the lashing blizzard.

"Dad, are you here?" called Matthew, once he got inside.

There was no answer. The gray house trembled in the freezing gloom. With shaking fingers Matthew flipped the light switch. Nothing happened. He tried another. Nothing. For this house, at least, the power had failed. He got one of the fat white emergency candles from the cupboard and lighted it and with the same match lit the propane stove.

Keep calm, he told himself. If you think this is bad for you, think what it must be like for Dad and Charlie out there somewhere in this storm.

He sat on his bed and stared into the candle's flame while outside it grew as black as midnight. A sudden draft of wind snuffed out the light. The door was flung open and two Mounted Policemen stamped the snow off their boots and shone their flashlights around the room. Matthew struck a match and relit the candle.

"All by yourself, are you?" asked the tallest one, taking off his fur hat and beating out the snow against his knee-high boot.

Matthew jumped. "Has my dad come back?"

"Not yet," the other policeman answered and looked worried. "That's quite a storm out there. But your dad's probably sitting safe and sound in an igloo Charlie built. The Eskimos taught him how to cut and shape the blocks."

"Charlie's good at it," the younger policeman said. "He builds a round snow wall, then pulls the engine tarpaulin over the top. I know. I spent a night out with him once myself."

The tall policeman laughed. "Sure, they'll be all right. This storm should pass by morning. Then you'll hear them whirling back in here shouting for hot food and lots of coffee."

The younger policeman looked at Matthew seriously. "Your dad did take food with him, didn't he?"

"I . . . I don't know," said Matthew, looking in the cupboard. "He had two chocolate bars in his big pack, and Charlie had sandwiches, I guess."

"Oh, they'll be fine," said the tall policeman. "I'm thinking about you. It's kind of lonely here in this cold house. Would you like to come over and sleep with us tonight in the police barracks? We've got a spare bunk."

"No thanks . . . I'm OK here."

"We may drop by later and see you, if the road stays open. But it's filling in fast. You sure you don't want to come?"

By ten o'clock Matthew wished that he had gone with them. He got in bed because the rising wind was sifting fine snow beneath the door and blowing it across the floor like icing sugar.

It was the worst night Matthew had ever spent. The bleak gray house trembled and bumped like an ancient ship as the wind blasted against it. Sharp crystals of snow rattled against the windows as though a thousand evil fairies scratched to find their way inside. He was haunted by the vision of his father crouching, freezing, unprotected in the storm.

Matthew got out of bed long before dawn. He lit the stove and made warm powdered milk. It was lumpy and tasted like chalk, but anything seemed better than lying in the lonely darkness seeing frightening visions of his father.

At 7:20 A.M. the storm door squealed open. Matthew heard feet stamping off the snow.

"Dad!" he yelled and, leaping up, jerked open the inner door.

"Sorry, Mattoosie. It's only me," said Kayak, beating the snow out of his parka. "I thought you might be kind of lonely, so I came to visit. *Pudluriapunga,* we say. I come visiting. See," he said, "my mother send you a nice fat piece of fish. Usually you send fish to a sick person. My grandmother says you're not sick, but still both of them worry about you down here all alone. They say you might be hungry. Did you have some breakfast?"

"No. I'm OK. I don't want any food just now."

"Well, you will when you smell this fish cooking. It's delicious."

Kayak went outside and brought in ice and chipped it into the pot. He chopped the frozen fish in half.

"The wind feels like it's going down," said Kayak. "Not so much snow blowing around. But it's still too bad to go to school today. The school is closed in this big wind. Teachers must be afraid the wind get in the hoods of little girls and blow them away." He laughed.

"I brought some playing cards," he said, spreading them out on Matthew's sleeping bag. "I teach you an Eskimo game called *Tidlimutlo koleetlo.* You got to learn to play it very fast."

The windows steamed up and the smell of fish soup

and biscuits filled the room.

"That burning biscuit smell is awful," Kayak said. "Why do you burn them black like that?"

"I like the taste of it, and the smell reminds me of my mother's kitchen."

Matthew ate like a starving man, feeling the warm fish soup spread through him. Somehow, he didn't feel like playing a game. He lay down on top of his sleeping bag and listened to the wind rattling at the windows.

"Get inside your bag and have a sleep," said Kayak. "Is it OK if I lie down here on your father's bed?"

"Sure," said Matthew and he watched Kayak shake out their small orange pup tent and pull it over himself like a blanket.

When they woke, it was late afternoon and deadly silent. Kayak coughed and sat up. Matthew could see his breath blowing out like steam. It was dark when they had finished eating.

"The wind's gone," said Kayak. "Come on. We go over to the radio shack and ask them if they hear anything from Charlie and your dad."

Outside the moon had risen. It cast eerie patterns of light and shadow across new snowdrifts that had blown down the roads and swirled high around the buildings. When they climbed across the new drifts, Matthew was surprised to find them so hard-packed that their footsteps scarcely left a mark.

"Oh, so you're young Matthew Morgan?" the radio operator said, when they got to the shack. He shook hands. "The police were over here last night, when the storm was at its worst and we had a ton of static on the set. We called south to let the government know the flight plan had been incomplete. We'll call again, if we read negative, till midnight. Then they can turn the problem over to Air Force Search and Rescue."

"Are they here?" asked Matthew.

"Hell, no," the operator said. "They're in Greenwood, Nova Scotia, about eighteen hundred miles southeast of here. Johnnie's been calling out every ten minutes since he came on shift at four o'clock and we've been listening on Charlie's band and on 500, the Air Force emergency frequency. But we're not getting any answers. Matilda's radio must be dead. In this country cold freezes up these flying machines when they're left sitting on the ground."

Matthew shuddered at the two words, "dead" and "freezes." "Can't you do anything?" he asked them in a shaky voice.

The radio operator smiled at Matthew. "Don't worry, son. When the Air Force Search and Rescue decide to come, they get here mighty fast. But the police have a plane on skiis over at Chimo. If we don't hear from Charlie and your dad, they will probably start a search sometime tomorrow."

It had not been particularly cold during the blizzard, but in the stillness that followed when the wind had died down, the temperature plunged to thirty-eight degrees below zero. That was —39 Celsius. Matthew went to school for half the next day, but could not concentrate on anything except his father out there somewhere in the frozen whiteness. Even the mountains that had been windblown with much rock exposed now stood like hunched white ghosts leering through the ominous blue shadows.

After school Kayak again came to Matthew's house.

"I'm glad my mom's not here," Matthew said to him. "She would hate these long days of waiting!"

"Where is your mother?" Kayak asked him.

"She . . . well . . . she was. . . . She died in a car accident in Arizona. She . . ."

"Oh," said Kayak.

Just then they heard a plane and ran outside the house. It was bright yellow with blue-tipped wings and tail.

"Mattoosie! It's the Mounted Police plane," Kayak called.

They heard the engine pitch change and watched it swoop toward them.

"They got ski wheels. They can land almost anywhere." Kayak held up his hand to Matthew. "Listen! Look down there. It's another plane. A big one." He shaded his eyes against the evening light. "It's the Air Force Rescue plane. Look! You can see the big search blisters shining on it's sides. Now they're going to find Charlie and your father. Just you wait and see!"

Together they ran toward the hangars, and when Matthew and Kayak reached the airstrip, both planes had landed. Two policemen in fur hats with blue parkas and bright yellow stripes on their trouser legs were walking in with the Air Force crew.

"This is Matthew Morgan," said the tall policeman who shook hands with the new arrivals. "It's Matthew's father who's sitting down out there with Charlie. They must be somewhere southwest of here, along the edge of the Grinnel Glacier. I'll show you Charlie's flight plan. Greenland Radio says they've got low clouds and bad weather coming in again."

Matthew felt sick about the flight plan. Should he tell them?

"Sir," he began to the policeman. "The flight plan . . . it's . . . it's wrong. They're further north. I mean, I think . . ."

"Oh, no," the policeman said. "Charlie knew where he was going. Try to relax. We'll find them soon enough."

The Air Force pilot nodded at Matthew, then looked at his watch. "It'll be dark in a couple of hours, and it will take us half that time to take on fuel. So we'll get a good night's sleep and start out at first light in the morning."

The police pilot glanced at Matthew and saw his tensed-up shoulders. "You want to come out with us in the morning, Matthew? We need all the eyes we can get on both sides of the plane. You can bring

your pal, if you want. Eskimos are super clever spot-
ters. They can see a white fox running on white
snow."

"I'd like to go, too, if you've got room," said
Johnny, the radio operator. "I'm off shift tomorrow
and I'm sick of hearing nothing. I need a little action.
I'd like to go on search with you and Matt and
Kayak."

"Good," said the pilot. "You tell the cook we'll need
lots of sandwiches and coffee. See you here tomorrow
at 0600 hours. Got it? Don't forget the sugar for the
coffee!"

Matthew saw the navigators unroll their maps as
they went inside the airport manager's office and
closed the door behind them. Beyond the door four
strange white men stood talking to the man from the
flight tower. Matthew could tell by their pile of gear
that they were the newly arrived mining men. He
turned and walked quickly away, not giving them a
chance to ask him any questions about his missing
father.

"My grandmother says you shouldn't stay all alone.
Come and sleep at our house," said Kayak. "You
bring your sleeping bag. We'll find my cousin and
ride up to Apex with him."

"All right," said Matthew, grateful that he would
not have to spend another night of waiting in the
lonely government house.

He rolled up his sleeping bag, slammed the door
and jumped aboard the snowmobile. It roared into

life and, leaving the road, zoomed across the hard-packed drifts. The icy rush of air seemed to whip all feeling out of Matthew's face.

When they stepped inside Kayak's house, a blast of accordion music and stifling heat and the smell of seal oil made Matthew's head reel. He turned, wanting to run out into the fresh air of the night.

"Throw your sleeping bag down there on my bed," called Kayak, sweeping his tangle of blankets onto the floor. "I'm going to sleep down here. I sleep my very best on a nice hard floor."

Kayak's mother, Elizabee, smiled at him and said, "*Ionamut,*" and a lot of other words in Eskimo.

Kayak translated. "She says she was sorry to hear about your dear mother, and she says it can't be helped about your father. She says sometimes our people get lost. Men hunting get lost. Sometimes they get back. Sometimes—well, that's what she say."

She pointed to the man who was playing an accordion. Kayak translated again.

"Parr got lost once, she says. He was gone for one whole moon in January."

Matthew saw the crutches beside the accordion player and saw that he had no feet.

An image of the great white bear, its mouth open, appeared in the room and hung there like smoke, reminding Matthew of the terrifying photo he had seen in the magazine.

"My uncle Parr says greeting to you, Mattoosie.

He's going to play a special tune for you, one his father learned from the whalers, when they used to winter on their tall ships frozen in the bay."

Parr started playing a sea chanty and soon after the old grandmother in the corner perked up and played her mouth organ. A little boy came and sat on Matthew's knee, and Kayak made funny faces at him. Matthew drank the sweet black tea and laughed with all of them, and for a little while he almost forgot about his father and his mother and his awful troubles.

Later, he said to Kayak, "When we go out with the plane tomorrow morning, I bet we'll find them right away. It must be easy to see that bright red *Waltzing Matilda* sitting up in all that flat white snow."

Kayak nodded his head, but did not answer.

Early the next morning, the old grandmother shook Matthew and Kayak awake. Matthew rolled up his sleeping bag, while Kayak woke his cousin who had slept on the floor near him. They followed their own tracks back to the airport in the snowmobile.

The engines of both planes were already roaring, warming up for the flight. Matthew watched with awe as the air crew and a dozen Eskimos boarded the big Air Force plane. It revved up its engines and thundered down the strip, rising like a silver gull. As it turned, he saw it reflect the orange light of dawn.

"Come on," said the police pilot. "I want to keep

visual contact with them. I don't like the look of those low clouds forming on the horizon. The last thing we need is another storm."

Matthew had a sick feeling in his stomach, knowing that they were probably going to search in the wrong place. He watched the snow race away beneath them and was surprised at how quickly the wide-winged Otter seemed to soar up into the air. They turned once around the airport and headed south into the Arctic gloom. Matthew saw the big Air Force plane's red lights ahead of them, blinking in the sky like a lonely Christmas decoration.

The navigator came back into the cabin and showed them a chart of the area south of the glacier.

"We will crisscross first, then start our grid search here," he said, and marked an X over the southeast square. "Keep your eyes wide open and alert for any strange sign that you may see. But every twenty minutes relax in turns, and close your eyes and rest. If you stare too long at blank white snow, you won't see anything. If the sun comes out, wear these dark glasses or you'll go snow blind. Shout out if you see anything and keep your eyes on it. Don't lose sight of it. OK?"

"OK," said Kayak. He, like Matthew, was already staring out the window.

"What's that?" cried Matthew, pointing.

"That's a rock," said Kayak.

"I suppose it's that rusty red color because its got iron in it," said Matthew.

"You'll see a lot like that," Kayak answered.

The crisscross of the glacier showed them nothing and slowly they began to fill in the squares. At nine A.M. they ate the sandwiches—everyone except Matthew. At ten o'clock the copilot walked back and stretched and said, "It's getting hard even to see the ground out there, there is too much drifting snow."

The copilot said, "Maybe tomorrow," and put his hand on Matthew's sagging shoulders. "It's a big country out there. It looks flat from over here, but flying above it you can see how it is made up of hills and gullies and a thousand little frozen lakes.

"I don't think we flew over the plane today. Charlie's got a broom with him. He and your dad would keep the snow swept off that bright red chopper, so we could see it from the air. And he's got a box of signal flares, they say."

Matthew's eyes felt dry, as though sand had been blown into them, and he was sick with worry. Should he try to tell them again about the flight plan being wrong?

Toward evening the storm lifted and another big Air Force plane, its wing lights flashing red over Frobisher, came in to join the search.

At first light next morning the three aircraft flew off the strip. Matthew and Kayak were with them again. There had been no chance for Matthew to speak of his father's flight plan. Everything was organized to get the planes off without any delay.

Following the search grid carefully, they checked off every square.

"Grid completed 1500 hours," he heard the pilot calling out on the intercom. "We have thirty-two minutes left for search."

The copilot came back, stretching stiffly.

"Matthew, Kayak, have you seen anything at all today?"

"No," said Matthew quietly. "Only that old plane wreck you pointed out to us."

"Have you any ideas, Matthew? Did your father say anything special to you before he left?"

"Yes . . . yes . . . he did," said Matthew. Now was his chance. "My father was afraid the new prospectors would read Charlie's flight plan and follow them. I mean my dad's sure he's found something important on the map. He showed it to me."

"Where on the map? You point it out for me."

He hurried forward and brought back his navigator's flight map. Matthew studied it.

"I'm not certain," he said. "This is such a different map. A different size. But I think if the weather was right for them, they might have flown up here." He pointed.

"That's outside our grid. "We'll have a look up there," said the police pilot. "We have a half-hour of fuel left and we can look over that part of the country on our way back to the base."

Matthew could hear him calling the Air Force

planes and saw them turn and follow. Their small police plane flew lower than the others.

Matthew looked at the Air Force grid chart. If only he had his father's colored aerial map with the green lines. If only he could read the contour lines on the map that marked the hills. Everything looked different covered as it was with snow.

As they headed for Frobisher, Kayak shouted, "I see something over there." He pointed out the window at the white expanse that lay north of them.

"I can't see anything," said Matthew.

"It's there, it's red," yelled Kayak. "It's Matilda. I'd know her anywhere!"

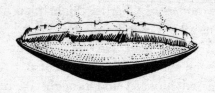

V

"KAYAK SEES SOMETHING," MATTHEW SHOUTED TO THE pilot.

"You too?" asked the pilot, looking back.

"No," said Matthew in a disappointed voice.

"Where was it?" asked the pilot.

"Out there," said Kayak, pointing west. "But I can't see it anymore. It's hidden by a cliff."

"Sorry we can't look for it now. We haven't enough fuel in our tanks. I'll ask the Air Force pilots to check the area on their way back to base."

Matthew heard him calling to the two big planes on his radio.

It was twilight when Matthew landed in the RCMP plane, and twenty minutes later, just before dark, the two Air Force planes came thundering down the strip and rolled in toward the hangar.

"We did three high turns over the area of sighting but didn't see anything except some windblown rocks. You sure you saw something, a helicopter? A red one?"

"I was sure," said Kayak shyly. "Maybe . . . maybe I was wrong."

As they walked inside, the pilot said, "How's the weather report for tomorrow?"

"Bad," said Johnny. "Bad all over Baffin Island. They've got a whiteout up north in Pangnirtung and the same condition west at Cape Dorset. And there's ice fog at Igloolik. We'll be lucky if we get a whole day's flying."

Overnight the weather turned warm and in the morning there was fog. Matthew and Kayak stood on the bleak airstrip at six A.M. They could scarcely see the big Air Force planes that seemed beached in the fog, like stranded whales.

"We'll let you know," said the man in the tower who was sipping cold black coffee. "I don't think anybody's going to fly today, do you?" he asked and pointed at the runway where it disappeared in drifting ice fog.

Matthew went back to the empty gray house. Unrolling his father's ordinary maps, he found the Southeast Baffin sheet and pinned it to the wall where it would catch the window light. He studied it carefully, moving inch by inch north, noticing how the hills were marked by red contour lines.

Elevation 200—300—400 feet. They were red. Yes, he could see the hills and he ran his fingers between them. These must be the valleys in between. The pencil trembled in his hand as he had a momentary vision of his father. His face was frozen white. Matthew closed his eyes and tried again, hoping desperately to remember where the green streaks had appeared on the colored aerial photograph. Finally he moved his hand forward and made three short lines on the map.

He whirled around when Kayak scuffed his feet. Kayak's eyes were red from two day's searching and he looked tired.

"I think that's where they went!" said Matthew, and he drew a small circle on the map.

Kayak studied the map, tracing his finger northward from the dot of Frobisher.

"*Ayii*," he said. "That's just about where I saw the red thing. It wasn't any rock I saw. It was red and sitting in a little gully by a cliff. Rocks are only showing on the hills where the wind has blown them clean. Let's go and tell the pilots."

"That's no good," said Matthew. "I've been over. They say they can't fly today. There's too much fog."

"*Ayii*, and no wind to blow it off," said Kayak. "Sometimes in spring it stays like this a week or more."

"A week?" Matthew moaned. "They'll be dead by then." He had to face the truth.

"How far away is that?" asked Kayak, pointing at the map.

Matthew held a piece of paper against the tiny scale. It showed twelve miles to the inch. He marked off eight inches and a little bit, then multiplied eight by twelve.

"Ninety-six miles," he said, "less than a hundred miles."

"We could go there on a snowmobile," said Kayak. "I've been to Kingmerok and back. That's farther. It was easy."

"Could we go now?" asked Matthew.

"No," said Kayak, and he paused to think. "Maybe if the planes can't fly tomorrow, we could go. But don't tell anybody. They would stop us sure! My cousin will go seal hunting with his father and they use his dad's big snowmobile. Maybe he wouldn't be too mad if I sort of borrowed his for a couple of days. We could find your dad and Charlie and bring them back here quick."

"That's great!" said Matthew. "What do we need?"

"About twenty gallons of gasoline," Kayak said.

"Here, I've got some money." Matthew pulled his wallet from his pocket.

"Good! I'll buy the gas," said Kayak, "and borrow my dad's .22 rifle and my grandfather's telescope. You get some food and the tent and pack up your sleeping bag and warm clothes. I'll bring you a real fur parka and some sealskin boots and mitts. Bring dark glasses. There'll be plenty of glare out there.

It's the worst time for that—in spring, in fog.

"If the planes can fly, we go with them tomorrow. You understand?" said Kayak. "We only go tomorrow ourselves if the planes can't fly. Want to come to my house?" Kayak asked.

"No, thanks," said Matthew. "I'll stay here."

Next morning Matthew was at the tower the minute it was turning light.

"Worse today than yesterday," said Johnny. His face looked gray.

Matthew could not even see the Air Force search planes standing out on the strip.

"I checked with Lake Harbour and Arctic Bay. This whole part of the island's blanketed with fog. I'm sorry for you, kid. I know you must be sick with worry about your dad. But there's nothing any of us can do but wait."

Matthew ran quickly along the road and as he came to the Government house, he could hear a snowmobile engine roaring. The sound was distorted by the heavy fog. In a minute, Kayak drove up on his cousin's Ski-doo.

"Tie your sleeping bag so you can sit on it," said Kayak, "just in front of that big red can of gasoline. I've got the gas tank full. You got the tent and food?" he asked. He checked his father's rifle to see that it was lashed on tight.

"I have," said Matthew. "Enough food for two days, maybe three."

"I'll help you lash it on this sled. We'll tow it behind to bring back Charlie and your father."

They worked together, quickly, quietly, their voices muffled by the fog.

"Put on your dark glasses and pull up your hood over your cap. Hang on tight, but be ready to jump clear fast. We're going down there," said Kayak pointing toward huge piles of jagged pressure ice along the shore. "Be careful. That's the kind of rough ice that broke my father's leg. We've got to find a path out onto the flat ice of the bay. This fog makes it hard to see. Hurry, I don't want some uncle of mine saying, 'Kayak, where you going with all that stuff packed on your cousin's snowmobile?' I'm no good at telling lies."

Kayak pulled the starting cord and the engine roared into life again. They ran down the long snow slope toward the bay.

The rough pressure ice was piled higher than Matthew's head. There were huge slabs of it heaved up by the daily force of the tide. So narrow was their passage that they had to kneel on the seat to protect their legs. As the snowmobile lurched across a deep crack in the ice, beneath him Matthew could see the icy blue-green water choked with slush.

"We're on the sea ice. Don't worry, it's about nine feet thick," Kayak called to Matt, as they huddled together. "We go that way," he said, looking back to see that their load was still lashed tightly to the small sled.

Matthew stared ahead, but saw nothing except a blank wall of drifting fog. Looking behind him he saw that the buildings of Frobisher had disappeared. So hard was the wind-packed snow upon the sea ice that they scarcely left a track.

They stopped at noon while Kayak relashed the sled, and between them they ate two pilot biscuits and shared a chocolate bar. Matthew ate some snow.

"Don't eat much of that," said Kayak. "It only makes you thirsty. Later we chip some ice and boil it into water."

They traveled on across the ice until they saw the moon shining weakly through the fog, lighting the ghostly hummocks that stood before them.

Kayak stopped the snowmobile and walked back to the sled. Matthew got off to follow. Kayak pulled a short hardwood staff out of the load on the sled. It had a piece of iron jammed into both ends.

"What's that?" asked Matthew.

"It's an old harpoon," answered Kayak. "The head and line are in my bag. I use its chisel end to feel the ice beneath the snow before I take a step. This is a very bad place."

He ran it two feet down until it struck hard ice. "Sometimes the snow hides wide cracks. If you're not careful, then you drown! You wait here," said Kayak. "We are across the bay now; there are dangerous tide cracks between the ice and the land."

Kayak disappeared in the fog. Matthew stood in

the silence waiting. When at last he saw the ghost-like figure of Kayak hurrying back toward him through the fog, he let out his breath in relief.

"It's going to be hard to get off the ice," said Kayak. "We got to be careful. No old tracks to follow. That snowstorm hid everything."

They got on the snowmobile and Kayak drove on once more through the fog, following his own faint footprints in the moonlight until they came to a high barrier of ice.

"The land's on the other side. Can you drive this snowmobile?" asked Kayak.

"Yes, I think so," said Matthew. "I've been watching how you do it."

"Then follow me. But go slow. I'm going to climb through that pressure ridge. If you feel that machine start to sink through the snow, you jump far away from it and lie flat, spread out like this." He held his arms and legs spread wide.

Matthew didn't like the sound of that, but he turned the handles until the machine inched forward, then eased the steering bars right and left to test the control he needed, and followed Kayak's path.

The first icy slope was broken in the middle by a long jagged crack, and as he passed over it, he could see black water beneath him. The crack was only a foot wide, but it had an evil look. Ahead of him Kayak climbed through a narrow gap formed by two chunks of ice as big as trailer trucks. On the icy downslope the snowmobile slithered sideways and the small sled bumped the back, and Matthew almost lost control.

"Come on, hurry," said Kayak. "I hate this hanging in the middle between the sea ice and the land."

Matthew had never worked so hard in all his life, as he struggled to force the heavy machine forward. Suddenly he heard the slowly turning snow track grind as though it would tear itself to pieces.

Kayak ran back and threw his full weight against its side and shouted, "Sharp rocks!"

Matthew jumped off and cut the engine and together they lay breathless against the machine.

"We made it," Kayak said. "We're . . . on the land."

Matthew saw Kayak snatch off his mitt and run his hand along the hard rubber links of the snowmobile's track.

"We loosened them right here, but they didn't break."

Cautiously Kayak gunned the motor and eased the snowmobile up the wind-swept beach. Around them, ominous black stones the size of crouching soldiers stood exposed. Matthew felt a light wind rising and saw it tear away the last remaining shreds of silver fog. Before him to the northwest lay the mountains gleaming in eerie moonlight.

"My grandfather used to say that right through

that gap," Kayak pointed upward, "is the best way through these mountains. In summer a river flows down there with many waterfalls. It is frozen now and should have enough snow on top of the ice to make a good winter trail."

"It looks hard to me," said Matthew, staring at the steep white cliff faces on each side of the narrow river's mouth.

"Who can tell unless we try," said Kayak. "You just pray with me," he said, "that the river ice is not blown clear of snow."

"We could put up the tent and sleep here," said Matthew. His muscles trembled with exhaustion and he hated the thought of the twisted frozen river hiding like a white serpent in the dark shadows of the mountains.

"No," said Kayak. "I'd be afraid to stay here. Feel that wind rising? You see how it has blown most of the snow off the beach? If that wind gets strong, it will tear your tent to pieces and kill you. I want to get safe in those mountains where we can hide from the wind. Come on, move fast. We go right now."

He gunned up the engine and Matthew sat close behind him. They made their way cautiously through a short roll of hills, hearing the engine echo off the slopes. They followed the frozen river course into the protection of the mountains. In the path of moonlight ahead of him, Matthew saw a cruel glint of ice.

"It's going to be bad at first," said Kayak. "But maybe better later. When we get through those mountains, I think tomorrow we find your dad and Charlie over that way. That's where I saw something red."

"You think the Air Force will be flying tomorrow?" Matthew asked him.

"I don't know," said Kayak looking up at the night sky and the moon. "The wind is from the south tonight. That may bring fog blowing off the open water. But we don't care too much about the fog," he said. "That's only bad for *tingmiaks*—for airplanes!"

Deep in the mountains they could feel the river sloping upward. Sometimes they avoided frozen rapids where ice had formed in rough bumps. It grew colder and the moon hid behind the steep white cliffs that stood on both sides of the narrow river. Matthew sat shivering on the snowmobile, his head buried deep in his parka. He watched ahead, past Kayak's fur-trimmed hood. He could see a frozen waterfall rising like a white-walled fortress against them.

"We're going to take a rest at the bottom of the falls before we try the worst part."

When they reached its base, Kayak shut off the engine. "I hate that noise," he said, as he stood up and stretched his arms. "I just want to go to sleep."

"Me too," Matthew mumbled. "We've been going more than fourteen hours." Together they took the tent and sleeping bags off the sled.

"We won't take time to put up the tent," said Kayak, as he unrolled his bag beside the snowmobile. "We can just wrap it under us and on top of us and sleep in our bags. That way we can go quickly in the morning."

They lay down and in an instant Matthew could see that Kayak was sound asleep.

In the utter silence Matthew peered around, staring into the ghostly shadows of the mountains. It was a dead world where no creature moved or breathed. But somewhere high above him he could hear the wind sighing through the mountain passes. The wind seemed to move the night stars on their lonely course, spinning each one, causing it to send out light signals that flickered bright as icy diamonds. So tired was Matthew that he saw no image of the white bear, as he pulled his sleeping bag and the orange tent over his head and slept.

Kayak woke him in the morning and, although they lay in shadows, the sky above them was a brilliant azure blue and the early sunlight lit the highest peaks with a glaring golden light.

"The planes should be out today," Kayak said. "Maybe we'll see them. Maybe they'll be there when we find your father."

Matthew was so warm in his eiderdown sleeping bag that he could scarcely force himself out into the snow.

Kayak broke a chocolate bar and gave half to Matthew. "You'll need all your strength today," he said, as he walked over to a rock face and snapped off a hanging icicle. "I don't want to take the time to light a fire," he said. "You suck a little piece of this for water."

They shared a small box of raisins and Kayak started to plan their course up the side of the frozen waterfall. He unhitched the small sled and packed all of their gear on it.

"The snowmobile will never pull this sled. We will have to go and feel the path for bad rocks and drag the sled up ourselves. Rest when you need to. Don't sweat too much. I'm going to check the gas tank first though."

Kayak unscrewed the gas cap, put a little stick inside and said, "*Ayii!* She needs gas very badly."

He untied the big spare can from the sled and for the second time since Frobisher filled the tank.

"Easier than feeding dogs," he said, as he screwed the cap back on.

They tied two lines to the sled and harnessed themselves to it like dogs.

When they reached the top, at last, they sagged against the sled exhausted. Matthew found that in spite of the cold his shirt was wet inside his nylon parka. He unzipped it.

"Be careful," said Kayak. "You'll get cold too fast. If you're too hot, you take off one mitt. That will slowly cool your whole body. When your hand gets cold, you put it back on quick."

Together they made their way back down the side of the frozen fall. Kayak gunned the snowmobile engine into life, but they did not mount the long black seat. They walked one on either side climbing the steep rough trail that they had made, each pushing as hard as he could.

When they finally climbed over the upper edge of the falls and drew up beside the sled, Matthew collapsed on his hands and knees in sheer exhaustion.

"Uggh," he gasped. "I never thought we'd make it."

"That frozen waterfall was the worst part of our trail, Mattoosie. We should be near the place where I saw the helicopter sometime this afternoon."

They slithered along the upper reaches of the icy river toward the lake that was its source. Matthew sat behind Kayak and stared in wonder at the mountains sheathed in snow and ice. Kayak wove the machine from side to side, trying to travel on every patch and drift of snow, avoiding ice.

"Look over there," he called.

Above the cliffs, Matthew could see the great white spine of the Grinnell Glacier humped like the back of some frozen dinosaur. Long spumes of snow were blowing from its western summit, whirling and shimmering like spun silver against a sky as cold and blue as tempered steel.

"There's a long lake out there in front of us," said Kayak. "*Tessikotak* we call it. From there we will see the highlands."

They struggled on until they reached the shore of the lake and relaxed as they crossed its smooth snow surface.

"There's a lot of wind out there," said Kayak, "but we're not so far from where I saw the helicopter."

They stopped and Kayak went back to the sled to draw his grandfather's old-fashioned brass telescope from its sealskin case. Matthew heard him groan and saw him fall to his knees and pound the sides of his head.

"What's the matter?" shouted Matthew.

Kayak did not answer. He could only point along the trail behind him. A thin, faint yellow-colored line strung out after them. It stretched across the whole length of the lake.

"*Peetahungitoalook!*" screamed Kayak. "It's all gone. Our gasoline's all gone. The cap came off. I tried to screw it tight, but it shook loose and came off on that damn waterfall!"

He leapt up off his knees and ran to the snowmobile, unscrewed the tank cap and measured.

"Gone," he wailed. "It's all gone. Just enough for maybe a mile—or two at most. And we're more than seventy-five miles from Frobisher. Maybe fifteen miles from where I think I saw the helicopter."

Just then a savage blast of swirling snow whistled along the lake and filled their hoods with wind. Behind them a huge snow slide rumbled in the mountains.

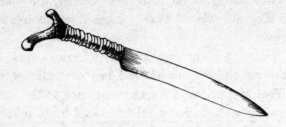

VI

KAYAK SLUMPED IN THE SNOW AGAIN. "I BRING YOU OUT here to try and save your father and Charlie, and what do I do? I get us both killed maybe. We got no gas. Only a little food. Look at that storm coming straight at us across the plain. See those big whirling wind giants with their snow whips searching for us. Can't you hear them howling out there, getting ready to freeze us in the cold?"

Matthew was as frightened as Kayak, but he went and stood beside him. "It's not your fault . . . The rough ice shook the gas cap loose. If it's anyone's fault, it's mine. You're risking your life to try and help me find my father."

Kayak stood up slowly and looked Matthew in the eye.

"It's too far to walk back with the storm coming. Our only chance now is to find them. There may be gasoline in the helicopter."

He took the lens caps off his grandfather's telescope and rested it against a rock. For a long time he said nothing, as he searched the wide plain carefully.

"There's something way over there in the blue shadow of that cliff," he said. "But with the snow blowing I can't make out whether it's Matilda or just an iron-red rock."

"Let me see," said Matthew, and his throat grew tight as he thought of the chance of finding his father and Charlie alive and well.

It took him a long time to find the small red smudge in the eye of the telescope. It must have been three or four miles away, and it remained a blur half-hidden by drifting snow.

Cautiously Kayak started up the engine and they moved out beyond the frozen lake.

"Go slowly," Matthew said. "That way the gasoline will last us longer, take us further."

He studied the snowmobile that was about to die. He wondered if there was anything worth taking from it. The seat cushion would be too heavy to carry. There was nothing else that they might want unless, perhaps, it was the rearview mirror.

When the snowmobile coughed and wheezed and finally halted, he took out the Swiss Army knife he carried in his hip pocket, unscrewed the mirror, and put it in his pack.

"What are you doing?" asked Kayak in disgust. "What good is that? You want to look in the mirror when you comb your hair and brush your teeth? You lucky if we stay alive. Remember, we're looking for your father."

"I haven't forgotten that," said Matthew, and for the first time he felt annoyed with Kayak. "You don't learn much living way up here, do you? Haven't you ever heard of Scouts or Apaches signalling with mirrors in the sunlight? I've seen them do it out in Arizona."

"We are not in Arr-ee-zon-a, and that mirror is worthless here," said Kayak, as he took up the telescope and searched the barren landscape. He pointed toward the dull red spot once again.

"I'll bet it's them," said Matthew, not because he really was sure, but because it was the only thing that might be a helicopter and he wanted desperately to try and reach it.

"I don't know," said Kayak, "but I guess we've got to go and see. Maybe if we're lucky and we walk fast, we'll get there before the storm closes in on us."

Kayak fumbled in his old canvas tote bag and pulled out a second pair of knee high sealskin boots that had a pair of thick caribou inner linings.

"Here," he said. "These should fit you. Put them on instead of those heavy boots of yours. Roll the orange tent up tight and tie it to your pack. I'll carry the two sleeping bags, the rifle, snow knife and telescope."

Kayak took the lashing off the sled and coiled it. "If it gets blowing really hard out there, we'll tie ourselves together. The worst thing would be if one of us would lose the other in the storm. I'll walk ahead and you stay close behind me. Yell if you get so tired you've got to rest."

Matthew put on the sealskin boots. They felt light and comfortable as slippers.

"Thank you. These feel great!" he said.

But Kayak did not hear him. He was already moving out toward the red speck that they had seen with the telescope.

Matthew had to strain to keep up to Kayak on the wind-hardened snow, but he didn't mind, as long as they were going toward the lost helicopter. Sometimes he even had to trot. Kayak's legs were short, but he seemed to glide over the hard-packed snow as sure-footed as a caribou.

Kayak looked back. "Put on your snow glasses," he said.

The sun had disappeared in the low white clouds that scudded over their heads. Everything was an indistinct blur. There was no horizon, just a frightening mist of blowing snow.

Matthew's shin muscles ached. A dozen times he wanted to cry out to stop, and yet he hurried on after Kayak, his head down against the wind, trying to place his sealskin boots in each one of Kayak's foot-steps, determined that they should reach the heli-copter.

A great winter blast came against them, causing Matthew to stumble to his knees.

"I can't!" he called. "I can't go on. Wait for me!"

Kayak stopped and hurried back. He crouched be-side Matthew for a moment. Then another blast of wind shook them, driving fine snow into their faces. It felt as sharp as broken glass. Kayak uncoiled the line and lashed it around his own waist, then tied the other end around Matthew.

"I don't go anywhere without you," said Kayak, trying to make a joke. "Come on, brother of mine," he said affectionately, "We have only a mile or two to go and then we find Matilda and Charlie and your dad. Keep your face turned away from the wind and follow me."

Matthew felt strong arms help him up and a gentle tug on the rope against his waist. His pack which had seemed light enough in the morning, now seemed to weigh as much as a huge gorilla hanging on his back.

He staggered along in Kayak's footsteps, saying to himself, "This foot forward . . . now this one . . . then this one . . ." He tried to think of something else, anything else, but no other thought would come to him in the screaming, eddying whiteness that slowly turned to gray as night came on. Only once he raised his head and saw Kayak walking beside what appeared to be a monstrous whirling snow devil. Far taller than a man, it seemed to poise on one toe like the shimmering specter of a ballet dancer, then moaning like a spirit, it disappeared in the hanging curtains of moving snow.

He could not tell now long they stumbled through the blizzard, but suddenly he tumbled onto Kayak's crouching back. Matthew knelt beside Kayak, holding his numb shinbones.

"Help me dig," gasped Kayak who hacked at the hard snow surface with the long blade of his father's snow knife. "Use your hands," he yelled. "Dig! Dig like a dog. The wind is getting stronger. We've got to hurry. Do you hear me, *hurry!*"

As he clawed at the snow, the one thing Matthew could see in the whirling whiteness was a stone. Its windblown tip stood black above the snow. It was no bigger than a dog.

"Find a guide rope from the tent and tie it to that stone," yelled Kayak in the howling blizzard. "Knot it tight."

When Matthew had managed to find a line and jerk one end of it free of the tent, he flung it around the rock. Then pulling off his mitts, he tied a granny knot and yanked it violently. It held. When he put his hands back in his mitts, his fingers were so stiff he could scarcely make them move.

He rolled into the hole that they had dug by the stone and tried to smooth the floor. Kayak had cut crude blocks of snow and had set them in a circle.

The wind howled over them like hungry wolves.

"Now," shouted Kayak, "unroll the tent, but hold on tight."

Having the main line anchored on the stone, they let the wind spread the orange nylon over the hole. Then hurriedly they lashed the other lines across some of the snow blocks. They caught and held, forming a trembling roof for them. After that the roaring wind seemed less violent.

As they lay gasping, a strange feeling of peacefulness spread over Matthew. He just wanted to go to sleep. Kayak kicked him with his foot.

"Unroll the sleeping bags," he ordered. "But wait, let me spread our parkas underneath. Take your pants and skin boots off, Mattoosie, before you get into your bag. I'll try to find our food."

In the blackness everything was difficult. Matthew wriggled until he managed to burrow into his down-filled bag. It felt icy cold.

"Take off your sweater and put it on your head," said Kayak.

Matthew did as he was told. He heard Kayak rummaging in the tattered canvas knapsack, taking out a candle and a package of matches.

"I hope you brought lots of matches," Kayak said.

"I don't usually carry them," Matthew answered, as he searched his pockets. "I . . . guess I . . . I . . . forgot to bring any."

Kayak moaned. "I have only these." He counted. "Seven . . . eight . . . nine left in the package."

"Then we have only those nine matches." Matthew winced.

"Only eighteen matches! Watch me," Kayak said, and, after borrowing Matthew's knife, he cunningly split one of the paper matches lengthwise with the thinnest blade.

"There now, we have two made out of one. But you must be very, very careful when you strike them on the package. My mother showed me how to make three matches out of one, but for that you need a razor blade."

Matthew blinked as the half match sputtered and flared in the darkness. He saw Kayak hold the thick candle stub to the flame, then drive his snow knife horizontally into the thick block wall. He tipped the candle sideways, dripping wax onto the handle of the knife, then stood the candle upright on it. The flame flickered, but it did not blow out.

"I'm starving," said Kayak. "I could eat a musk ox."

"Me, too," said Matthew, and he held a pilot biscuit over the candle and sniffed the smoky smell of burning flour.

They shared and devoured their only tin of frozen corned beef. "This meat will make your body hot. You'll give off heat into your sleeping bag. Go ahead," he added, "suck a little snow, if you are thirsty."

He looked up at the orange tent stretched flat and quivering above their heads. "Not too bad a house," he said. "I hope it holds till morning. We'll let this fat candle burn. You'd be surprised how much it will help to warm our little place."

He reached over and patted Matthew on the shoulder. "You're pretty tough for a *kaluna* boy," he said. "You're like an *Inuk*, a real man. You don't complain. That's an awful storm out there. To tell you the truth, Mattoosie, I mostly lived in our house in Frobisher. Not since I was small in my grandfather's camp did I ever sleep out in a storm like this. But my father takes me out hunting often on the ice, and he teaches me the things his father taught him. Eskimos never used to go to school you know. Kids just learned everything from their father, mother and grandparents. That's the way it is still when we're out living on the land."

Kayak was right about the weather. When Matthew awoke, the orange tent glowed in patches above his face and the whole world seemed deadly silent. Pulling them out from beneath them, they wriggled into their parkas, pants and boots, all of which they had kept dry beneath their sleeping bags, and Kayak cut a new exit passage in the low snow wall. They crawled out.

Everything had changed. Piles of snow were whipped like stiff meringue into high wavy drifts and the spring sun made the whole plain sparkle to the flat horizon in the north. Above them the blue sky hung like an endless dome marred by not one single cloud.

They worked without mitts to pack the sleeping

bags and tent, for it seemed almost warm.

"Spring is coming fast," Kayak joked. "This whole tundra plain will be covered with flowers—yellow, white, purple—beautiful! We'll soon be bitten by mosquitoes. Put on your dark glasses. A day like this can burn your eyes and make you snowblind," he warned.

He squatted by the rock and examined the horizon with the telescope. Kayak said, "See the blue shadow of the cliff way over there? We try that first. We'll keep the rising sun off our right shoulders. That way we'll be walking straight north."

The walking was more difficult because the new snow was loose and soft beneath their feet. It was afternoon before they reached the gully by the hill. But there was nothing there but an endless waste of snow.

Now Kayak took his rifle off his pack and carried it across his shoulder. He seemed to be searching for something. Matthew felt his stomach cramp with hunger and he wished that he had saved his raisins to eat them one by one.

"Mattoosie," said Kayak, pointing into the north. "We go to that little valley way out there. If we do not find them today, we will have to turn back. The caribou have moved. There's nothing to eat out here."

He was wrong. Just before evening he made a quick sign to Matthew and knelt down. He cocked the .22 rifle and took careful aim. All Matthew saw was one black spot upon the snow. It was no bigger than his fingernail. He saw the spot blink, then heard the rifle fire. He saw a white form leap in the air, then drop and kick, then stiffen.

Together they ran forward and Kayak picked up a big, plump Arctic hare.

"Oh, Mattoosie," he said. "This *okalik* is going to taste delicious. He came here as a gift to save our lives. Maybe he makes us lucky."

Matthew gladly carried the hare and they went as quickly as they could to the narrow valley. They found nothing except a curving line of footprints.

"What made those?" asked Matthew.

"*Amahok*—a wolf! A big one!" answered Kayak, as he examined the line of tracks. "I hope he's far from here by now. Maybe by now the Air Force found your dad and Charlie."

"I can't go back without finding them!" Matthew groaned.

"It's the only thing we can do," Kayak said.

Dog tired they stumbled on into the night. Once more they dug a hole and raised a low snow wall, drew the tent over it and tied the lines. Kayak squatted on the snow and skinned the hare and cut it into quarters. Once inside he lit the last candle.

He offered Matthew two sections of the hare and showed him how to hold its flesh over the candle. "This way," he said, "it will sort of cook a little and get warm." He laughed and turned his back to Matthew and ate his raw.

"This rabbit tastes kind of like rare chicken," Matthew said, his mouth jammed full. "Do you think tomorrow we can get another one, or two, or three?"

"No," said Kayak. "We were lucky to get this one. There's others hunting out there, too. Those big snowy owls and white weasels, they don't miss much, wolves and white foxes find the rest, and . . ."

He stopped speaking and listened. At the end of the valley there was the long, lonely howling of a full-grown Arctic wolf.

"I hate that sound," said Matthew, gobbling down the last of the hare as though he wanted to keep it from the wolf. "It sounds like coyotes out in Arizona, only worse."

Kayak listened to the second howl in thoughtful silence.

"My grandfather says the wolves won't hurt you unless they're starving."

"That wolf sounds starving to me," said Matthew.

"Well, don't worry. He won't come tonight. Wolves are afraid of a light at night."

Kayak laid the rifle down between them, ready. They huddled in their bags and tried to go to sleep.

"Mattoosie, are you asleep?" Kayak whispered.

"No," said Matthew. "I keep thinking about tomorrow night. We'll be out of candles then. We won't have any light to keep that wolf away."

"We think of that only when the time comes. We're alive. We got food in our bellies. We're not sick. You be glad of all those things, Mattoosie. To-

morrow is tomorrow. We see what happens then. Tonight we go to sleep!"

In the morning the sky was silver gray. There was
no horizon anywhere. The size of every object in the
landscape seemed distorted.

"Bad today," said Kayak. "No sun to guide us. No
stars. Easy to get lost and walk in circles. I don't
know how we look for your dad today in this whiteout."

Everywhere there was an eerie silence.

"I'm going to yell," warned Matthew as he cupped
his hands around his mouth. "Dad! Charlie!" he
yelled. "Dad! Charlie! Where are you?"

The echo came back to them along the valley.
"Dad—Charlie. Dad—Charlie. Where are you?"

The lonely sound of his own voice frightened Matthew. It made the world around them seem like a
frozen echo chamber.

Kayak once more flung the sleeping bags upon his
back and turned south, "Come on! It's no good. We
can't stay here. We got to go. Right now. We've got
to try for Frobisher. We got to get back home."

"I've got to find my dad! I've just got to! He's the
only family I have!"

Kayak turned and looked at Matthew. "No, you've
got me," he said. "I'll be your brother. That makes
you part of my whole family. They care about us.
They're waiting for us to come home soon. My mom,
she'll be glad to have you for a son. She'll take good
care of you if you feel sick and when she sees your

worn-out mitts, I know she's going to make you new ones.

"And my sister Pia, you'll like her. She's always laughing, smiling. She'll probably sew up my ripped parka. She's good at sewing.

"You cheer up, Mattoosie. It looks like winter but spring is coming soon! Our dad, he'll take us both out fishing with him. You should see him fishing! You'll see, he knows a hundred times more than I do. He can be your teacher too. See, Mattoosie, you have got a whole new family now.

"Anyway," said Kayak. "What do we know wandering around out here. Maybe your other dad and Charlie are back in Frobisher by now."

Kayak carried the rifle across his shoulder. Matthew followed him, head down, still feeling that he was deserting his father. Together they walked for five hours, stumbling sometimes, because the whiteout showed no edges on the drifts of snow.

"There's something there," said Kayak eagerly. "Man-made."

He ran forward, with Matthew after him.

"Oh," he wailed, and went down on his hands and knees. "It's ours. It's the hole we dug last night. The house we left this morning. We've walked in one big circle," he cried, looking up at the blind, sunless spread of clouds. He shook his head. "My father warned me about doing that. I've been a fool." He held his arm across his eyes to block out the cruel glare of the whiteout.

They sat together on the crumbled snow wall.

"What can we do?" asked Matthew.

"Nothing right now," said Kayak. "Only sleep here again until night, then pray it is clear. With the North Star to guide us, we can walk all night."

They went to sleep in the afternoon, but that night the weather was no better. They slept again, with nothing to eat and no candle to warm their shelter.

Next morning fog lay everywhere in great patches. Near their tent they saw the broad footprints and the yellow urine stain left by a big male wolf.

"The same one," said Kayak. "He must be very hungry to come as close as this. He's starving maybe —waiting like us for the caribou to come."

For a few minutes they stared at the tracks saying nothing.

"Let's go. If we hang around here and wait for something to happen we'll only get cold and sick," said Kayak. He pulled on his parka. "We'll pack up this camp forever. I know a way to go straight away from here and not turn circles. It takes work, but it's what I should have done before!"

Every few hundred paces Kayak cut a long thin snow block, stood it up and pulled some dark deer hair from his parka trim and punched it into the center of the snow block like a bull's-eye on a target.

"We go only as far as we can see that mark," he said, pointing back, "and then, we build another one. That way we don't get lost."

In three hours they had erected maybe twenty

blocks, when suddenly in the white haze that hung before them, they saw a big gray-white crouching shape. It crept toward them, it's teeth bared. It stared at them with cruel yellow eyes.

VII

"IT'S THE WOLF," SAID KAYAK. HE RAISED HIS RIFLE TO shoot, but it turned and slunk away into the fog. Kayak ran after it with Matthew following.

They must have gone half a mile, when suddenly Matthew heard Kayak yell in terror and disappear from sight. Matthew hesitated only for a second, then ran forward to help. But the fact that Kayak had disappeared made Matthew cautious.

It was good that he moved forward slowly, for suddenly an icy canyon yawned at his feet. He had to throw himself back to keep from falling.

Looking down, he could see a terrifying tumble of sharp rocks and deep crevasses engulfed in mists.

He heard a moan, and a few feet below him he saw Kayak clinging to the icy rock face. With one foot he was frantically searching for a foothold.

Swiftly Matthew jerked off his pack and pulled out one of the long nylon tent lines. He lay down and with his head and shoulders hanging over the cliff, tied the line securely around Kayak's left wrist. It was the only part of Kayak that he could reach.

Kayak did not speak, but Matthew could hear him gasping with the strain.

Matthew leaped up and ran away from the edge. He ran as far as the tent rope would allow and then stamped and dug himself knee-deep into the hard packed snow, making himself like an anchorman in a tug of war.

"Start climbing!" he shouted. "I'll pull as hard as I can."

He felt a tremendous weight come on the line, and he heard the nylon tent rope stretch, as Kayak released his grip on the cliff. Matthew watched the rope fearing that it would break.

With all his might he pulled and gained a yard of line. So heavy was the weight on him that the snow beneath his feet began to give. But he hauled again with every ounce of strength that he possessed.

Kayak's fingers emerged above the cliff face and dug like a desperate pair of crabs. They must have found a hold. For an instant the line went slack and Matthew hauled a man's length of rope, then set his weight against it and saw Kayak's head and shoulders appear. He hung there like a dying man. Then with Matthew's steady pressure on the rope and one enormous heave, Kayak lunged his weight forward. He lay gasping on the edge of the icy rock, his legs still dangling over the abyss.

Matthew pulled the rope up snug and called to Kayak. "Crawl toward me."

Kayak did not have the strength to, and Matthew feared that he might slip back if he released the tension on the rope. He worked slowly forward, straining madly until he was close enough to grasp Kayak by the hand. Cautiously he hauled him away from the cliff face back to safety.

They both lay on the snow, unable to move after their tremendous struggle.

Kayak was the first to speak. His voice was trembling. "I lost the rifle and the snow knife and my dark glasses. All of them are gone. I could hear them fall. They hit the rocks a long way below."

Matthew went forward on his hands and knees and looked down at the base of the cliff.

"There's an enormous split in the rocks down there," Matthew said. "It's almost like a long deep cave. The rifle and the knife are gone. The harpoon, too. And our tent . . . it's torn in half."

"Come on," he said, as he unbound Kayak's wrist and helped him to his feet. "The main thing is that you are still alive and safe. We have to get around this cliff before night comes—and we've got to stay together!"

It was a long time before they found a way around the cliff face and were once more on the plain. It was snowing hard again. Kayak's left arm hung at his side as though it had been pulled out of its socket. But when Matthew asked him about it, he only shook his head and said, "From now on we're in bad trouble."

What would it be like, Matthew wondered—no igloo walls, a torn tent, no light, no heat, no food. He could feel his own hope running out of him as they stumbled forward across the endless snow. They had come looking for his father, and now they, themselves, faced death. Kayak who had always broken trail for them was now staggering a hundred feet behind.

In the gray light of evening Matthew saw a movement on the snow before him. He wanted to call to Kayak to bring the rifle. Then he remembered that it was lost.

The thing he saw crouching on the snow before him was dark in color, not a hare or a fox. Could it be a wolverine?

Suddenly the thing turned and stared at him. It appeared to be a human head with no body—just a head, with tangled hair and eyes as wild as a frightened pony. A chain of teeth dangled from its heavy brow.

I'm going crazy, Matthew thought, as he watched the head twist round and disappear.

"Kayak!" he gasped and, turning, saw that he was close beside him. "I saw a man's head right there on the snow!"

"Hunger is making you crazy," Kayak mumbled.

"Hunters sometimes see strange things out here."

"Look over there," whispered Matthew. "There's another one."

Kayak wiped his hands over his eyes. "I saw it! The face, I mean. It ducked down very fast."

"It wasn't the same one I saw before," said Matthew. "That one was smaller."

"Look, another!" Kayak whispered. "Can't be real people. Must be *tornait*—evil spirits."

"The big head's up again," said Matthew pointing at it, and he crouched like a sprinter ready to run away.

"*Kenookiak?*" said a deep rumbling voice.

They could see its teeth.

"*Inootweenak,*" answered Kayak. Then to Matthew quietly he said, "The head asks who we are. I said we're humans—only humans."

"*Shoonamik peeumaveet?*" the head shouted.

"*Kakpoosi,*" answered Kayak. "The head asks what we want. I said we're hungry, starving."

"*Kilee, kilee,*" growled the head.

"It tells us to come forward. I am so afraid," whispered Kayak.

"What can we do?" asked Matthew.

"Nothing," answered Kayak. "Except go forward."

Rising cautiously, the two of them walked toward the head. It disappeared.

When they reached the place where it had been, they saw a hole in the snow, and looking down into it, they saw a pair of wild eyes staring up at them.

"Don't stand there like two stupid stones," a voice bellowed in English. "Come down here!"

"I'm not going down into that hole," said Kayak. "That thing speaks every kind of language and will bite my legs off."

"I'm coming down . . . sir . . ." said Matthew timidly.

He paused, listening. Out of the hole he heard a voice singing. "Well, come on, boy. What's akeeping you, hoo, hoo, hoo, hoo!"

Matthew lowered himself into the hole, and he felt a powerful pair of arms grasp him round the waist. A voice below him in the darkness called out.

"I caught one of them. Here, hold this one, woman. I'll get the other!"

Matthew felt someone grasp him by the parka hood and haul him through a dark passage into a dimly lighted room. He could see several silhouettes moving in the shadows.

Kayak came tumbling after him into the room.

"Two of them," growled the deep voice. "That's not a bad day's hunting in these parts."

"Why, they are nothing but a pair of poor lost boys," called a woman's voice out of the gloom, and she cackled like a goose. "This one's a *Kaluna*. He's got a red face and yellow hair. But that one, he's an *Inuk* for sure."

"What's your name, boy?" asked the big rough voice. "Where you come from?"

"Frobisher," said Kayak. "This is Mattoosie. My

name's Kayak. We are looking for Mattoosie's father and the helicopter pilot, Charlie. Our snowmobile ran out of gasoline. Now everybody's lost."

The wild man looked at his wife and laughed. "That's why we heard those airplanes buzzing around up high, searching, I suppose, to find his daddy. Well, he aren't around here, boys, or I'd know it. Wouldn't I?"

Matthew stared through the gloom, trying to decide whether he was in a round house that had been built above the ground or in a strange natural cave beneath the earth. He could see a foot-long yellow line of flame wavering and burning like a dozen candles on either side of the room. Everything else lay in shadows. Just above his head were the curved rib bones of ancient whales supporting the roof. They gave him the eerie feeling that he was inside the body of a living monster.

At least half of all the round room space was taken up by one great bed that seemed attached to the back wall. On top of this bed was a tumble of animal furs, army blankets, and every kind of clothing. Many curious metal objects caught the faint light and winked and glowed from the walls like shining teeth. A small boy slept upon the bed.

Matthew drew back when the wild man stared at him. He had shaggy hair and small quick eyes set above his prominent cheekbones, and a jaw so powerful it looked as if he could crack the thigh bones of a bear. When he moved his head it set teeth bound around his forehead to rattling. His parka, pants and boots were made of caribou skin, and he had many little magic bags and symbols hanging round his neck and sewed onto his parka sleeves.

He snorted and said, "This is the land where I live. I don't welcome strangers. We've never had a visitor since we came here, have we, woman?"

"Only caribou and the bear," she answered, pointing at its bleached skull and shaggy hide and a pile of antlers.

"Have you always lived out here?" asked Kayak.

"I tell you, NO!" exclaimed the wild man. "I used to live in Frobisher. I was born there. That was before, when it was called *Ikhaloweet*. Before the allied Air Forces came. There was only one white man who traded foxes there in those days, and he had an Eskimo wife. It was a lovely place for fishing, and the caribou used to come right down to where we camped beside the river.

"Everything's changed now," he said. "I hate that noisy place—buzzing with trucks and airplanes. Some Eskimos act crazy there. No wonder."

"That's what my grandfather used to say," Kayak said.

"Well, he's right," yelled the wild man. "What was your grandfather's name?"

"Tytoosie," answered Kayak.

"Oh, I knew him." The wild man laughed. "I liked his ways. A fast dog team driver and a fine hunter. He had a son named Toogak."

"That's my dad," said Kayak, sounding proud.

"Well, why do smart people like your family still live in a crazy place like Frobisher, crowded with people, like walrus clinging to a tiny rock. Why don't they spread out and hunt, enjoy the country like I do, like all our people used to do?"

"I don't know," said Kayak. "Almost everybody talks about leaving. But nobody does it. Maybe they'd feel lost out here—like us. If we hadn't found your house, I think we would have starved to death."

"Stop talking about dying," said the wild man's wife. "You drink this nice hot soup," she said, passing each of them a battered tin bowl marked "U.S. Army."

Matthew felt a great dizziness when he tasted the rich delicious brew and felt its steam against his face.

The woman drew two caribou legs from the pot and split them with a heavy knife.

"Go ahead," she said, "Reach in and get yourselves a nice chunk of meat. Eat slowly," she warned, then laughed. "If you eat too fast when you're hungry, it will make you throw it up."

When they were finished eating, Kayak sat back upon the bed. Matthew's head nodded forward.

"Lie down and have a rest," she said, rolling one of her sleeping children sideways to make room for Matthew. "Talking can come later. You sleep now." She flung two blankets over them.

When they awoke, it was dark inside the house, but a bright curve of light through the entrance hole made Matthew know that it was morning. Kayak was already sitting up, carefully picking at a caribou bone with a borrowed knife.

"Mattoosie," he said, waving the bone. "This is *putik*—marrow." He held up a soft delicate piece, then popped it into his mouth. "It's the best food in the world. The *kalunas* mostly throw it away. Here, you try some."

It was warm from the pot and seemed to melt in Matthew's mouth like soft butter.

As the light inside the house increased, Matthew could see that the red eyes that had glared at him from the walls were the reflectors off old military jeeps and trucks, and the shining teeth were metal grills from freezers. Above the woman's head and glowing in the light from her oil lamps were many rows of empty, colored-glass bottles and the walls were covered with hundreds of pictures pasted every which way, many of them upside down and on the ceiling so that you could study them while lying in bed.

When the wild man saw Matthew staring at the pictures, he snorted like a horse and said, "Most things the white men make are junk." He pulled back his sleeves and on each arm he wore half a dozen wrist watches. "I pull off the hands," he shouted, "because I don't want white man's gadgets telling me anything. I only want the sun and moon to tell me when to wake and sleep."

Suddenly the wild man rose and standing on his

tiptoes stuck his head outside the entrance in the roof.

"*Ayii*," he bellowed. "*Silachiakpalo*. It's a good day. Quick, woman, give these boys a feed of meat and they'll be on their way. Don't let us hold you up, travelers. Your boots are dry. My wife has chewed them soft for you. Put them on. Get going. Hurry. Go!"

"Well, we thought we might stay a . . ."

"I tell you this," the wild man said. "If you promise to leave right now, I'll give you three good presents. The first—this bow with arrows. It's a spare one. Look," he said, and reaching behind him and fumbling in the bedclothes, he drew out a long plastic bow and quiver. It was double curved and laminated and still had the price tag hanging on it—$29.95!

"There," he said. "Brand new from the PX—that's the US Army store. And here's the nice green quiver full of arrows. If you don't know how to shoot it, get out there fast and LEARN!"

His wife started cackling again like a hen about to lay some eggs.

"I took archery at school," said Matthew. "Come on, Kayak, we'd better go."

"Hold, boys," the wild man whispered. "Don't rush away without my second present. Here's a snow knife and some flesh of caribou. My third present is the most important. I'm going to show you how to get back home to Frobisher. And if I see your daddy wandering on the hunting grounds, I'll tell him where to go as well. Now quick as foxes, up and out you get!"

"Not before I give them these," the wife screamed, and she hung a braided sinew necklace around Matthew's neck. "There," she said, "these charms will help you find your way and keep you warm at night."

Matthew looked at his gift. On the braid was strung a bird's bill and a bear's tooth and a little leather bag stuffed with something lumpy and sewed up tight.

She handed Kayak a pair of bone goggles of the old-fashioned Eskimo kind. "You broke your fancy glasses, *ayii?*" she said. "Well these are *Inuit* and strong. You wear them. Don't go snowblind like my brother."

Matthew felt a burly pair of arms around his waist, as he was hoisted through the roof hole. Kayak came tumbling after him.

The wild man's head appeared above the snow. He nodded and pointed with his nose. "Go that way, walking straight for half a day. You will come to a curvy little river frozen solid. Follow it until you come to a waterfall that flows so fast it doesn't let the water freeze. You'll see the fog a-rolling high in the air. Looks like it's coming from the devil's kettle spout. Where the river splits in two, you take the good arm," he said, waving his left arm in the air. "There's lots of wild white chickens with furry feet eating frozen berries by that stream."

He flung the plastic bow and quiver toward them

and as they slithered across the snow, he yelled, "Good-bye, boys, and don't come back. You hear me? 'Cause you won't find us here. Your coming means I've got to move. I mean, when you get back, you'll tell all the noisy folks. You'll say, 'We met a really different family living way out yonder!' And they'll start to look for me, 'cause white people can't stand the idea that I and my family are out here living FREE. You hear me? FREE! They'll want to stick needles in my arms and send my children off to schools to learn to be like them instead of me.

"Go ahead," the wild man shouted. "Tell them anything you want, because by the time they come here searching, we'll be gone from here. You hear me? GONE!"

He laughed and blinked his eyes and ducked his head beneath the snow.

Kayak and Matthew trudged south toward the distant river. Behind them they could hear the wild man banging on an empty honey pail and singing an Eskimo song, as though he didn't have a care in all the world.

"At first I thought he was crazy," Kayak said. "Now I'm not so sure."

"He's crazy all right," said Matthew. "Why would he tear the hands off his wrist watches?"

"Maybe he just likes the way they look on his arms . . . I mean, all shiny gold and silver," Kayak said. "We lost the time two days ago when your watch stopped, and now your watch can't find it for you.

Why don't you throw it away?"

Matthew looked at his watch. "I couldn't just throw it away. But I'd trade it for a one-cent box of matches."

Matthew could not tell how many hours they walked before they saw the fog rising from the river where it stayed open below some rushing falls.

"There it is," said Kayak, "like he said, the devil's kettle."

The sky was turning gray when they reached the hole kept open by the falling water.

"I'm going to have a drink," said Matthew. "I'm tired of eating snow." The water looked too cold to dip up with his hands, so he knelt on the shore ice beside Kayak and drank directly from the river. At the bottom, he thought he saw something shiny. "What's that?" he asked Kayak. "Can you see it shining down there in the gravel?"

"I don't know," said Kayak. "Maybe some little yellow stones."

Matthew pushed up the right sleeve of his parka shirt and sweater as far as he could and, lying on the ice, reached down into the water.

"Wahh! You're acting crazy," whispered Kayak. "You freeze your arm off, freeze yourself to death!"

Matthew could just touch the yellow pebble with his fingertips. He rolled it loose and caught it, as he felt the water seeping into his clothing. He pulled his arm out of the river. It turned numb as the cold air struck it.

Kayak snatched off his own hat, rubbed Matthew's arm and pulled down his sleeve.

"What are you doing?"

Matthew did not answer, so intensely was he studying the yellow pebble in his hand. It was almost as large as a sparrow's egg.

Suddenly they felt a rush of air above their heads and looking up saw a snowy owl swoop over them. Its curved talons were hooked as though to strike. The big owl landed on an upturned piece of ice not twenty paces down the river, ruffling out its feathers as a threatening warning signal. Matthew heard it hiss and snap its beak as it glared at him with tiger-yellow eyes.

He knelt down and slid the big bow off his back. Carefully he notched an arrow to the bowstring, and, taking steady aim, he drew it back full force. The big bird thrashed its wings in rage.

Crack—Whunk! The laminated bow broke in his hands, sagged toward him and collapsed, dropping the arrow at his feet.

"Did you try to kill that owl?" gasped Kayak. "Maybe the charm that woman gave you was strong enough to break that bow. Oh, you are lucky that bow fell to pieces. If you had harmed that owl, we would never leave this place alive."

"This fancy looking plastic bow was so brittle from the cold, it broke. That's all. No magic. It just snapped in half," said Matthew.

Kayak blew out his breath. "No magic? My grandfather knew owls. He would have told you that owls can speak like men. He would warn you, 'Never, never shoot an owl!' Look!" said Kayak, pointing at the angry bird.

The ice beneath the white owl's feet began to flash and glow like flames in the dying rays of the Arctic sun.

"I tell you, that owl is full of magic," whispered Kayak. "See how he has set his frozen perch on fire to warn you."

"I don't believe it," Matthew whispered back. He edged cautiously along the river until the big bird gave an angry hiss, rose and flew away on silent wings. Matthew moved toward the block of ice where the bird had perched.

"There *are* flames burning inside that block of ice," he called to Kayak. "I can see them blazing. I see frozen fire!"

Matthew picked up a chunk of ice and flung it boldly at the owl's sparkling perch. The ice struck the shining surface and, while Kayak watched in horror, it shattered into a thousand pieces.

Matthew raced to where the flaming owl perch lay in ruins. Kayak watched as he squatted down and picked up something, cautiously examining it in the evening light. Suddenly he jerked his penknife from his pocket and, with its point, stabbed and hacked at what had been embedded in ice. Kayak ran to Matthew's side.

At first Matthew did not speak. He only pointed

down into the river's gravel bed.

"There's a big one! And another there! And hundreds more caught in the ice and scattered over the whole bed of the river. Kayak," he whispered at last, holding up the shining pebble to show the long bright scratch his knife had made, "this is soft metal. Feel its weight. See how the earth's fire has melted them. These," he waved his hand over the river, "these are all nuggets of pure gold!"

VIII

"THAT OWL WAS JUST PLAYING A TRICK ON YOU." KAYAK snorted. "That's not real. That must be fool's gold. Our teacher told us about that."

"It *is* real gold, I tell you," Matthew shouted, as he made another wide knife slash across a second nugget and held it up to make it flash and glow in the remaining light. "Fool's gold is sharp-edged and too hard to scratch. Real gold is soft, like this! The ice block the owl sat on must have picked it up from the gravel bed beneath the water. This is placer gold!"

Matthew ran along the edge of the open water to a shallow place where the gravel riverbed lay just below the surface of the icy river. He waded into the water and stooping, picked up one, two, three of the nuggets. He scratched the largest one and let out a shout.

"It's all *gold!* Real *gold*, Kayak. There's lots of it. Look, there and there. We're rich, I tell you. We'll be *rich* forever!"

Kayak walked cautiously along the riverbank and saw the nuggets gleaming dully in the gravel at his feet. He did not stoop to pick them up.

"I've got a dozen already," yelled Matthew, holding out his freezing hands.

He began stuffing the wet nuggets into his pockets. He stared at Kayak who stood motionless, watching him.

"You don't really understand," Matthew said.

He bent and picked up a nugget the size of an olive. He bounced it in his hand and said, "This one weighs maybe four ounces. And gold is worth about one hundred and thirty dollars an ounce. Four times one hundred and thirty is . . ." He paused. "Five hundred and twenty dollars. How much did your cousin's snowmobile cost?"

"Nearly a thousand dollars," Kayak answered.

Matthew stooped and picked up another nugget that was slightly smaller. "There," he said, tossing the two nuggets to Kayak. "Those are a present from me. Go buy yourself a brand new snowmobile."

"Where?" said Kayak. "I don't see anyone selling any snowmobiles or any gasoline around here."

"Oh later, dummy," Matthew said. "Have you no imagination?"

Matthew went on snatching gold nuggets from the river. "I wish my dad were here."

"You're the dummy," shouted Kayak. "We're about to die out here unless we hurry, and you're in there getting wet and grabbing little bits of stone."

"Look at this one!" shouted Matthew, and he had a crazy look in his eyes. "It's huge. It would pay your way to fly around the world and let you eat all the best food every day . . . I mean, cakes and pies and ice cream."

"Never mind the ice cream," Kayak commanded. "You get out of that river and help me build a snow-house or the wolves will pick the ice from off our bones. See this one little piece of flintstone," said Kayak, picking it up from the riverbank. "How much is this worth?"

"Nothing," Matthew answered. "See this—this is gold!"

"Maybe this flintstone is worth much more than that," said Kayak and he put it in his pocket.

When Matthew left the river it was dark. Together they built the house against the newly falling snow.

"This is a terrible time of year," said Kayak, as they ate the food the woman had given them and huddled in the blackness without heat or light.

Even in his sleep, Matthew kept talking wildly about the treasure in the river and the wolf.

In the morning Kayak awoke and he found himself alone. He scrambled out the entrance. Down in the river he saw Matthew, shuddering with the cold, as he searched in the freezing water and tried to fill his pack with gold.

"You stop that," shouted Kayak. "We've got to go, right now. You can't carry a load like that."

"Oh yes I can," said Matthew. "Who could leave a fortune in gold behind?"

"I could and you should, too," yelled Kayak.

He hefted Matthew's pack. "You won't get very far with that."

"You watch me when it comes to carrying gold."

By noon Matthew was struggling along in Kayak's trail, a hundred feet behind, and by evening Kayak had built their igloo by himself. He squatted, waiting, until he saw the white boy's figure staggering up to him.

Matthew fell to his knees, as Kayak helped him to remove the heavy pack of gold. Matthew's face was covered in cold sweat.

"You can't do that another day," said Kayak. "You make us go too slow. After tonight we'll have no food. You'll kill yourself."

"Well," Matthew sighed. "I can't just leave this pack of gold behind. What would my father say?"

"I told you back there that you were like an *Inuit,* an Eskimo. But now I tell you you are acting like a crazy *kaluna.* I can't help you, if you're going to be like that."

They ate the little bit of food they had left and went to sleep without another word.

In the morning when Kayak woke, Matthew was gone again. Kayak saw him half a mile ahead staggering along the riverbank. Kayak overtook him easily and was about to move ahead, when Matthew spoke out in a shaking voice.

"Won't you take the pack and help me carry the gold? It's worth a fortune. We'll share it—half and half."

"No! NO!" said Kayak firmly. "I won't carry those crazy stones one step for you."

He heard Matthew sigh and saw him slip one shoulder painfully from beneath the packstrap, then let the great weight fall. He looked at it sadly.

"Come on," said Kayak. "I'll help you dump them. They're nothing but a load of worthless stones out here."

"I'm afraid we'll never find this place again," said Matthew, staring at the pile of gold that lay scattered on the snow.

"I never want to find this bad luck place again," said Kayak. He had to pull Matthew away, for he seemed hypnotized by the precious metal.

Finally the spell was broken and they headed south together.

That night Matthew's tiredness and his hunger gave him awful dreams. He screamed out loud when he saw the great white image of the bear.

The food was gone, the gun was lost, the bow was broken. Matthew and Kayak made their way slowly south along the frozen river toward the mountains.

When they stopped to rest, Kayak said, "A human is just like a lamp or a stove. If you put in fuel, it lights up and is warm. If you don't feed it, the fire goes out! My fire is dying I tell you. I can feel it slowly dying."

But they staggered on through the cold gray twilight of the Arctic afternoon. At night they built a tiny snowhouse and crawled in like two tired dogs.

"Sometimes I think that wild man told us the wrong way to go," said Matthew. "Sometimes I think we're still walking in circles."

"No," said Kayak. "I kept those two mountains straight ahead of me." He pointed. "When we go through, we should see the long arm of the sea. You walk right behind me in my footsteps. We reach the mountains by tomorrow."

The next day a cold sharp wind blew against their backs and seemed to drive them forward. Matthew was so hungry he felt light enough to take off and sail across the snow. They entered the mountains just before darkness came and hurried through a long valley.

"Just a little further," Kayak called to him. "I want to build our igloo right up there."

When they reached the height of land, darkness had come.

Kayak ran to Matthew and gripped him by the arm and shook him. "We did it! We did it!" he whispered.

Matthew could not tell if Kayak was laughing or crying.

"See over there. Across the bay. See the glow of lights? That's Frobisher. That's where we came from!"

Far away on the horizon Matthew could see a faint yellow glow in the sky, as though some strange moon was about to rise.

"I wonder if my dad is over there?" said Matthew. "Let's keep on going!"

Matthew took a step forward, but his legs bent like spongy rubber that might let him down at any moment.

"No, no," said Kayak, "That glow must be thirty miles away." He drew the long snow knife from his pack. "We'll build an igloo here and sleep. We'll feel stronger in the morning."

They left at dawn and traveled down the long slope toward the frozen bay. When they finally reached the ice, Matthew felt light-headed.

Kayak squatted in the snow and taking the broken half of the bow that he had saved, he lashed the snow knife to its grip.

"Why are you doing that?" asked Matthew.

"See that black fog rising way out there?" said Kayak. "The ice has changed. It's broken open. When we get out there, I'm going to have to feel beneath the snow for open water. I don't trust moving ice. You walk only in my footsteps," he added, as he carefully probed the ice before him. "Hurry," he said. "See that crack up ahead. It may be opening. It may be getting wider."

They ran toward the blue-green line that zig-zagged like a frozen streak of lightning across their path. To the south, Matthew could see a great green shining lake where the seawater had flooded over the ice.

"Too wide for us to cross," exclaimed Kayak.

He hurried north along the edge of the crack. Matthew dreaded the look of the black water that stood gaping before them, sometimes eight feet, sometimes twelve feet wide.

"We'll never get across that crack," said Matthew, and he felt like falling down and weeping on the snow.

"Come on," said Kayak. "Hurry! We've got to keep on moving."

The crack stretched like a long ragged tear in a piece of white paper for as far as Matthew could see.

"There's a seal," whispered Kayak.

Matthew saw a head as round and black as a bowling ball floating in the icy water not thirty paces from them.

"Oh, I wish I had my father's rifle," whispered Kayak. "Here we are, helpless, starving, and all that meat and fat staring at us. Even if I had the harpoon."

As though it had heard the dreaded word "harpoon," the seal's head ducked beneath the ice and did not reappear again.

"If it was summer, we could swim across like seals," Matthew muttered.

"Swim?" said Kayak. "Even in summer that water is so cold it would kill both you and me in a few minutes. What did you learn in school in the south? I mean in Aree-zona and British Columbia and Mex-ico?"

"Reading, writing, geography, history and archery and tennis. They were more fun."

"That's what I learned at school, too," said Kayak, "but no archery or tennis. Which one of those subjects is going to help you now, Mattoosie?"

"I don't know. I don't think any of them will help us."

"That's true, they won't," said Kayak. "Did they teach you about ice in school, Mattoosie?"

"No, not about ice."

"A *kaluna* once told me my grandfather was ignorant. You hear that? Ignorant! But everything we do right yesterday, today, tomorrow, comes from my grandfather. You'd be dead, I'd be dead already, without the knowledge of my grandfather.

"Today the subject is ice!" said Kayak. "Moving ice. And tides. Those two can kill you. So today we travel by my grandfather's school. He could only count to twenty—using his fingers and toes. He died thinking the world was flat. He knew spirits moved the ice or stopped it moving. He said on moonlit nights sometimes you can see the little people lying on their backs beside the tide cracks, scissoring their legs in the air and hear them screaming and laughing, teasing the poor humans. Would you say he was ignorant, Mattoosie? Ignorant?"

"No, he was not," said Matthew. "He understood the ice. Your grandfather never spent a day in school and yet today he is my teacher."

"Look there," Kayak pointed. "There is our only chance."

Matthew saw his friend run forward and kick hard at a four-foot chunk of ice that had cracked away from the main ice and then frozen fast again. Carefully Kayak knelt and cleared the snow away. Then seeing the weak fault where the ice pan had refrozen, he started chipping with the snow knife at the crack.

"Help me," he called to Matthew, who opened the largest blade of his Swiss Army knife.

Kneeling, they worked desperately. Small chips of ice flew up their sleeves, melted and ran along their arms in icy rivulets. Suddenly with a soft swoosh the small pan of ice let go and drifted. Kayak caught it with his knife and slowly drew it to him.

"I'll go first," he said, cautiously putting one foot on the ice pan.

Matthew saw it shudder and sink a little.

"It should hold me," Kayak said.

As though he trod on eggs, he carefully eased one knee and then the other onto the trembling pan of ice.

"Now push the ice," he said to Matthew. "Not so hard you'll tip me in, but hard enough to float me over to the other side."

Matthew lay on his stomach and with both hands he gave the ice a steady push. Kayak was on his hands and knees. A light breeze whipped across the ice and caught him like a sail, so the ice pan turned half around. Matthew closed his eyes and prayed.

"*Nakomik*, thanks a lot," he heard Kayak shout, and when Matthew opened his eyes, he saw Kayak scrambling onto the strong ice on the other side of the widening crack.

Kayak then began to chip two holes in the ice pan about four inches apart. He worked downwards in a V shape until the two holes touched. Then he forced the piece of tent line through the ice and tied it tight.

"Get ready," he called to Matthew and, pushing the ice with his foot, sent it drifting back across the crack. "You're heavier than I am and that ice is very tippy even though it's thick," shouted Kayak. "You be mighty careful how you climb onto it."

With the deadly cold black water all around him, Matthew felt like an elephant balancing on a cold round ball. Slowly, cautiously, Kayak drew Matthew toward him across the widening gap between the heavy shore ice of the bay and the great central body of ice, until Matthew, too, could crawl onto the strong ice.

If the two boys could have seen where they were going from an airplane, they would not have been in such a hurry to cross that deadly gap, for the ice in the center of Frobisher Bay was broken into a dangerous jigsaw puzzle of slowly moving pans of ice, rising and falling as much as thirty feet on the huge tides pulled by the terrifying forces of the moon.

"I think we're going to be all right now," Kayak called to Matthew. "The wind should make it easier to get onto the shore ice across the bay near Frobisher."

He was wrong. Dead wrong. For the next six hours they hurried across the vast broken ice fields, driving the knife in before taking every step, testing. Kayak warned Matthew a dozen times to step only in the footprints that he, himself, had made.

In the late afternoon they watched with terror as the huge tide flooded the ice, creating deadly lakes just south of them. With each step Matthew imagined he could feel the broken ice beneath them moving south toward the Hudson Straits where they would be swept to certain death in the North Atlantic Ocean.

As darkness came again, Kayak squatted on the ice and placed his head in his hands. He was trembling, and Matthew could not tell whether it was from cold or hunger or fear.

"It's no use going any further," said Kayak. "I can feel it, we are being swept away. The tide is carrying us too far south. We will never reach the other side."

"What do you mean?" said Matthew, horrified.

"See that hill," said Kayak. "It was far to the south of us this morning, when we crossed the tide crack.

Now it is so far to the north I can scarcely see it. We have moved fifteen miles south already. By morning we will have drifted thirty, almost forty miles away. We are lost, I tell you. Lost forever. Look. Look how the ice has split." Kayak showed him. "We were once on pans a mile square in size. Look how all of them have broken. You could not walk fifteen paces now without falling into water. I am sorry, Mattoosie, we are truly finished."

A cruel blast of wind swept out of the north, driving chilling swirls of ice fog around them.

"We must build an igloo," said Matthew, unlashing Kayak's snow knife from the broken bow.

"It is too difficult out here," Kayak mumbled. "The snow is wet with salt water."

"Still we must try our best," said Matthew, and he paced out the small circle as he had seen Kayak do and began to cut the thin damp blocks. Big wet flakes of snow came driving on the wind.

"Come and help me," Matthew called to Kayak.

"Don't move," answered Kayak in a whisper. There was terror in his voice.

Cautiously Matthew turned and saw the white head and black beady eyes as it moved snakelike through the icy water. When it reached the small ice pan on which they stood, the huge polar bear heaved its bulk out of the water and shook itself like an immense dog. It looked yellow against the stark white snow.

Matthew saw the great bear swing its head back and forth, sniffing the air suspiciously. Its huge blue-black mouth hung open showing its terrible teeth. With a rumbling growl, the giant bear lowered its head and came shambling toward them.

IX

MATTHEW AND KAYAK LAY LIKE DEAD MEN ON THE ICE, both their heads turned so that they could watch the bear. Matthew clutched the snow knife like a dagger and trembled inside, as he felt the wet salt water seep up from the snow and soak his clothing.

The bear did not even pause to look at them, as it stalked past. They saw it crouch down flat against the snow.

Cautiously Matthew looked ahead and saw a seal's dark head poised alert and motionless in the water. The bear was watching it intently.

Seeing nothing move to frighten it, the seal relaxed and let its back float to the surface as it drew a large breath of air into its lungs and dove beneath the ice in search of food.

The bear snaked forward cautiously until it

reached the very edge of the ice where it had seen the seal. It reached out its paw and scratched against the ice.

The seal must have heard the sound beneath the water and, being curious, it once more raised its head above the surface. Seeing nothing but a yellowish heap of snow, it swam cautiously along the edge of the ice.

Suddenly, with lightning swiftness, the bear's right paw shot out and struck the seal's head a killing blow. The left paw lunged forward and hooked the seal inward with its great curved claws. Using its teeth, the bear easily hauled the hundred-pound seal up onto the ice pan.

Matthew watched it sniff the dead seal all over, then roll it on its back and, holding it steady, tear its throat open with its powerful jaws. It started to devour his prey.

"Stay still," Kayak hissed through his teeth, now chattering from cold and fear.

At last Matthew saw that the big bear was finished eating. They watched it as it licked its lips and, like a huge cat, carefully wiped the seal fat from his mouth. It turned and shambled toward them, paused and sniffed the air. With its belly rumbling, it padded once more to the edge of the ice and slipped silently into the freezing water. Kayak sat up carefully as the bear swam south. They saw it climb upon another pan and amble off, disappearing into the whirling snow.

Kayak rolled stiffly onto his hands and knees, then crouched like an animal, still watching the place where they had last seen the bear.

"I'm soaking wet." He trembled. "Get up," he called quietly to Matthew. "We're in trouble now, worse than we've ever been before."

The north wind seemed to press its freezing hand against Matthew's soaking clothes. It glazed them with a thin white sheath of ice as stiff as armor.

"Being wet will kill us sure," said Matthew, shivering like a dog. "What will we do?"

"I don't know. We'll have to think of something," said Kayak, and he went forward and felt inside the seal.

In the half darkness Matthew saw him cut the big artery, then pull its heart out and set it on the ice.

"Quick, we got to build a shelter. Work hard and it will warm you up a little. Move your arms and legs," Kayak said, "so your clothing won't freeze stiff."

On one end of their pan, sheets of ice the size of tabletops lay scattered like playing cards forced there by the pressures of the rising tides. Kayak stood three upright, leaning them against each other. Then together they hauled two more into place to form a rough circle.

"Now gather snow," said Kayak, kicking it into wet piles with his soaking boots. "We'll chink up the holes and cracks between the ice to make it strong.

If the house blows down with the wind tonight we could never build a new one in the dark."

When their crude shelter was finished, it looked like nothing but another miserable pile of ice.

Kayak hurried away and returned with the frozen heart and the torn remains of the seal. He dragged them inside the little ice cave.

"It's just as cold in here," said Matthew. "We've only built a grave for ourselves."

"Unless we make a fire."

Kayak took the last matches carefully from his pocket and felt them. "They are soaking wet," he groaned, "and their heads have come off. Useless," he said and flung them on the snow.

"Then we can't make a fire," cried Matthew through his chattering teeth. "We've got no lamp, no matches, and everything is soaking wet."

He saw Kayak take the snow knife and hack white chunks of seal fat from the inside of the carcass and set the frozen heart up in the snow like a small melon with its top cut open.

"Give me your little knife," he said and with it he trimmed a narrow piece off the back tail of his shirt in a place where it was still dry.

"I hope I didn't lose it," Kayak said, searching his pockets with his freezing hands. "I've found it. My little piece of flintstone." He handed it to Matthew. "Hold it carefully. Don't drop it. It's worth more to us than gold."

Matthew had to help Kayak cut open the freezing front of his parka, so that he could reach into his inside breast pocket to get the little carving file and the wad of fine steel wool, the ones Matthew had seen him using in school.

"They're soaking wet," said Kayak. "Feel in your hip pockets. They're still dry. Can you find any pieces of lint or string?"

"Only just this bit of string," said Matthew. "Nearly nothing."

"It may be enough. Roll it into a loose ball," Kayak said. "Now, Mattoosie, you do everything exactly how I tell you. If you get your hands a little bit burned, don't mind it, understand me?"

Matthew wanted to laugh at him or cry. "How are you going to burn my hands? They're almost frozen."

He watched as Kayak struck the flint along the steel teeth of the little file. On the third try sparks flew into the wet steel wool and Matthew gasped in surprise, as he saw the fine steel wire spark and began to flare red and burn. The fire fizzled out.

"Now," said Kayak. "If I can light it again, you put the dry string in the spark with your finger. Do it right! My hands are freezing."

He struck the file again a dozen times before the steel wool sputtered into running sparks. Matthew held the wad of string against the tiny flame.

"Hold it there. Don't let it go out."

Kayak took the shirttail wick that he had made,

rubbed it with seal fat and held it in the tiny glow.

"Don't breath on it just yet," he said, and waited.

Matthew felt a blister raising on his finger.

"Don't move it," Kayak ordered.

Slowly the seal fat sizzled, then a real flame burst into life. Kayak blew gently on it, then carefully stuffed one end of the wick into the well of glistening seal fat that he had stuffed into the open cavity of the frozen seal's heart. The white candlelike flame expanded, as the seal fat softened and soaked upward into the homemade wick. Working as painstakingly as a surgeon, Kayak spread the cloth wick with his knife until the flame widened. He let out his breath in satisfaction when he saw that there was at least three inches burning hotly. The ice shelter reflected the joyful light. Matthew held his hands out, spreading his stiffened fingers in the life-giving warmth.

"I would never have believed that," Matthew said quietly. "That you could make a lamp stove out of a frozen seal's heart and make wet steel wool burn. It smells good," he said, "Like my mother's burning toast!"

"It's something," said Kayak, "I didn't learn in school."

With Matthew's knife he cut strips of rich red seal meat from the carcass where the bear had scarcely touched it. Together they warmed the strips over the little lamp and ate them. Matthew thought that he had never tasted anything so good.

"Now come on," Kayak demanded. "We go out of here and run around this little house as many times as you have fingers on your hands and I have toes."

When they came inside once more, Matthew felt warm all over as though the seal meat in his stomach was fuel on fire within him. His face and hands seemed to burn in the strong warmth and flickering light of Kayak's clever lamp.

Kayak unrolled the sleeping bags which were only a little damp.

"Tonight we sleep resting on our knees and elbows," he said. "The snow's too wet to lie down."

Kayak pulled off his parka and beat it with the piece of broken bow until the sheath of ice fell away, then he put his parka on backwards.

"Why are you doing that?" asked Matthew.

"Because I'm going to pull up my hood and breathe into it. That way I catch all my body heat. You do the same. It's a trick I heard about from my mother's relatives. It might help to save our lives."

In the first light of morning, Matthew heard the ice grinding and had the uneasy sense that their whole house was slowly turning. Kayak pushed out the piece of ice that he had used to block the entrance.

"Look up there!" he yelled at Matthew.

Matthew, still crouching stiffly, looked up and in the sky saw a long thin white contrail.

"It's the big plane," said Kayak, "going into Frobisher Bay or maybe over to Greenland. No use waving your arms," he said in a discouraged voice. "It can never see you. It must be two miles high."

Matthew whirled around, dived back through the entrance, reached into his pack and leaped outside holding the snowmobile's mirror.

"Give me the knife, the knife!" he shouted.

With its point he scratched a small cross in the mercury behind the glass. Then, standing in the rays of the morning sun, he placed it against his eye and sighted on the plane. Through the tiny opening he could see it moving through the cold blue sky like a slow silver bullet. He tipped the glass back and forth, back and forth, back and forth. He continued to watch the airplane through the hole until it was out of sight.

"What's that? Some kind of magic you are doing?" Kayak asked him.

"No," answered Matthew. "It was nothing, I guess. My dad told me that sometimes a pilot can see a mirror flashing from a very long way off. You know, it's that old Indian trick."

"Well, it didn't make them turn around," said Kayak. "They're all just sitting up there warm and dry and comfortable, drinking coffee in the sky."

"I guess you're right," said Matthew, and he dropped the mirror in the snow.

"The ice, it's breaking in half," screamed Kayak. "Quick!"

He grabbed Matthew by the arm and forced him

to jump across the gap. As they watched, half of their shelter broke apart and slipped into the freezing water.

"The sleeping bags and pack are gone," cried Matthew, and he lunged toward the edge to grab the heart lamp and the seal remains. He felt the ice pan tipping, as he slithered forward.

X

"NORDAIR FLIGHT TWELVE. NORDAIR FLIGHT TWELVE TO Air Control Frobisher. Calling Air Control Frobisher. Do you read me? Over."

"Frobisher Air control to Nordair Twelve. I read you loud and clear. Come in please."

"Our location is thirty-seven miles southeast of Frobisher. We have sighted a signal out on the ice at 10:24 A.M. The flashing appeared to be in distress sequences of three-repeat-three. We could see no object on the ice and it may have been the sun glinting off the water in the tide cracks. But it appeared to be a human signal seen by both the pilot and myself. Have you anyone reported missing? Repeat—anyone reported missing?"

There was a pause, and another aircraft signal interfered with his.

"I couldn't hear your answer, Air Control. There's static. We are estimating to be on the ground at Frobisher at 10:52 A.M. Will hear your answer then."

A steady wind blew out of the north and the cold spring sun glared off the snow-covered ice. They pumped their feet and swung their arms about their bodies to keep their blood circulating. Matthew watched the tide go slack, then turn, as the ice moved north again, but the north wind was against them and all too soon they felt the pull of the outgoing tide carrying them toward destruction in the open sea. Just before evening they saw a snowy owl pass over them, gliding, then beating its short wide wings, searching for they knew not what. The sun lingered, walking crablike along the western hills across the bay, then disappeared.

The cold that comes with night swept in and with it ghostly vapors rising like steam between the cracks of broken ice. The full moon rose, staring at them like a dead man's face, and once more they heard the dreadful grinding as the tide rose and drove them south with awesome force. Matthew closed his eyes and saw the image of his father and thought what he would give to see him once again.

Hurriedly they took the few pieces of flat ice that had not slipped into the water and once more tried to build a shelter, though it was scarcely big enough to house a wolf. When they had finished stopping up the holes with soggy snow, Kayak stepped up, pulled off his wet mitt and solemnly shook hands with Matthew.

"I wish we had known each other for a longer time," he said, "but I . . . I'm going to say good-bye to you now, Mattoosie."

"Oh, don't say that." Matthew spoke in a choked voice.

"Why not?" said Kayak. "What is going to be— will be."

He started to pull the last remains of the seal into the crude little house and then suddenly changed his mind and began to circle round the house, pressing down hard, leaving a dark red trail of seal blood in the snow.

"Now you're trying magic, aren't you?" Matthew cried. "What good will that do?"

Kayak didn't answer him. The only sound was the moaning of the ice in the gathering gloom. Together they crawled inside and huddled side by side, and ate some seal meat.

"Aren't you going to light the lamp?" said Matthew.

"Maybe later. What's the use? . . . Oh, I'll try to light it, if you want me to."

They slept, crouching like animals in the lamp's faint glow, until the first light of morning filtered faintly through their icy shelter.

"What's that?" gasped Kayak. He cocked his head and listened.

"I don't hear anything," said Matthew. "Wait! Wait! Yes, I do. I do!"

They kicked away the thin ice door and scrambled out the narrow entrance.

"Thug-thug-thug-thug-thug!" They heard a helicopter's engine driving the whirling blades through the glittering ice fog overhead.

"Oh, God, please let him see us," shouted Matthew.

"*Takovunga, takovunga!* Look at me, I'm here! Right here!" screamed Kayak.

"Come back! Don't go away!" they yelled together, waving their arms.

"It's going! It's going. It can't see us in the fog," said Kayak. "And we were in the house."

"Thug-thug-thug-thug-thug!"

"It's turning! It's coming back!" Matthew shouted and danced upon their pan of ice that was now shaped like a broken marble tombstone.

Suddenly the red helicopter loomed through the fog, hovered like a giant bird, then swept toward them. Like a pair of partly frozen scarecrows they danced a jig together.

"It's Matilda!" Kayak yelled. "It's the *Waltzing Matilda*. She's all patched up on one side."

They could see Charlie in the gleaming blister, waving at them wildly. One door of the helicopter slid open and Charlie flipped out a short rope ladder with metal rungs. Kayak staggered across the ice pan and grabbed it.

"I'm too weak to climb," he screamed at Matthew.

"I'll help you," Matthew shouted, and with his last remaining strength he heaved Kayak onto the dangerously swaying ladder.

"Get in!" Charlie shouted over the roar of the engine.

Kayak grabbed Matthew by the hood of his parka and helped pull him up the ladder. Matthew slumped down behind them. There was very little room inside.

"You two all right? Feet not frozen? No bones broken?" Charlie shouted.

They shook their heads.

He reached across Matthew and slid the door closed, then gunned the engine. *Waltzing Matilda* whirled up above their little ice shelter. Kayak looked down for the last time at what had almost been their grave.

Charlie pointed down and said, "Whoever made that red circle around that ice shack of yours certainly saved your lives. I would never have found you without that red bull's-eye. Where did you get the paint?"

"It's not paint," said Matthew. "He thought of the idea." Matthew nodded toward Kayak. "He saved us."

"It worked like magic," Charlie shouted. "And where did you get the mirror? The one you flashed at the Nordair flight that was coming into Frobisher. If they hadn't seen that mirror shining, we'd never have found you. The aircraft and the rescue teams were looking for you inland. That mirror saved your lives!"

"He thought of that," said Kayak. "Mattoosie saved us with his Aree-zoona Indian trick."

"There's lots of people who are going to be mighty glad to see you two. I imagine you could use a good hot meal. Here," he said, and handed each of them a chocolate bar.

Kayak's hands were so weak and trembling from the climb that he had to tear the wrapper with his teeth.

"Is my dad OK?" asked Matthew.

But Charlie had his earphones on and was speaking excitedly into his microphone and did not hear the question.

Matthew felt light-headed as he looked down and watched them rise through the dangerous ice fog. Beneath them spread the deadly puzzle of broken ice widening into dark open water to the south. He had never felt so glad to be away from any place in all his life. In the cabin's warmth his head nodded forward and he fell into an exhausted sleep.

Twenty minutes later Kayak reached out and put his hand on his friend's shoulder. "Look, Mattoosie, there's Apex, there's my house," he said, pointing, his mouth full of a second delicious chocolate bar. "I never thought I'd see my family again. I think that's my sister Pia and my mother standing out in front. And there's my dog!"

The bright red helicopter whirled in toward the airport.

"And there's our school," said Matthew.

Kayak turned and looked at him. "I never thought we'd have a chance to go to school again."

The helicopter landed in a whirling haze of snow crystals. Charlie turned off the engine and the big black blades stopped and hung silent in the harsh Arctic light of morning. Matthew could see a stream of people running out of the hangar toward them.

Charlie slid open the door and Kayak stepped out. He collapsed onto his knees from exhaustion but, taking hold of one of Matilda's big rubber helicopter floats, he lifted himself up and helped Matthew down.

"Be careful," he said. "You probably feel as weak as I do."

Together, supporting each other, they staggered toward the hurrying people.

"There's your dad," said Matthew, and his throat felt dry. "Where's mine?" he whispered, and he felt sick inside.

He turned back to ask Charlie and saw him hobbling painfully after them on a cane. The sight struck terror into Matthew's heart. He knew there must have been a bad accident. Matthew saw Kayak's mother hug her son, then whisper something in his ear.

The young policeman and a nurse and Kayak's family helped the two boys across the airstrip. When

Kayak's cousin smiled at them and held open the door, Matthew felt like he was coming home. Inside the airport he was sure he would see his father. But when he looked around, the whole big room was hot and empty. He felt his knees buckle under him, and he slumped down onto the floor.

Kayak sat down suddenly beside him and put his arms around his shoulders and said, "Everything's going to be all right." But Matthew could see that he had tears in his eyes.

"Just you two rest there," the airport manager said. "I've called the hospital. The ambulance is coming now. I can hear its siren."

When Matthew awoke, he turned his head and stared out the window. It was night. Beyond the lights of the airstrip he could see a long way down Frobisher Bay. Where he and Kayak had been, there was now only a sea of blackness. The full moon glowed like a mysterious spaceship sailing through the clouds spinning a path of silver across the mountains and the open water.

He looked the other way and saw Kayak who was sitting up in the neat white hospital bed, eating a bowl of chicken soup. He stared at Matthew. His face looked gaunt and thin.

"If I ring the bell," Kayak said, "the nurse will bring you something to eat."

"Where's my father?" Matthew asked in terror,

then placed his hands over his ears, for he feared to hear the answer.

The door opened and the nurse came in.

"Where's my father?" he asked again, and his voice was trembling so that he could hardly speak.

"Do you feel strong enough to stand?" the nurse asked quietly.

"Yes, I think . . . I can," said Matthew.

"Then put on your slippers and your robe," she said.

"Can I come with him?" said Kayak.

The nurse hesitated.

"I can help him walk," said Kayak. "We often help each other. He's in my family. He's sort of . . . well, he really is my brother."

Kayak's father, Toogak, was sitting just outside their door. He got up when he saw them.

"*Aneeioungilateet,*" he said to his son.

"*Aneeioungilateet,*" Kayak answered, and Toogak limped down the hospital corridor after them.

At the end of the hall the nurse opened a door cautiously, then said, "You can go in now. But you can't stay long."

Matthew had to hold onto Kayak, when he first saw his father lying in the bed. He looked old and tired, as though his big strong body had given out on him. His eyes were sunken, and there were black frost patches on his cheeks and forehead.

"Oh, thank God you're safe," his father said to

Matthew and grabbed his hand along with Kayak's. "You two boys never should have come out looking for us, and yet. . . ." His eyes had tears in them. "I'm so very proud you did."

"What happened to you, Dad?" Matthew asked, when he could speak.

"I'll answer for your father," said Charlie, who had come through the door behind them. "When I tried to take off from the base of the cliff where we had landed, the wind swept us in too close and we sheared off one of Matilda's blades."

"I thought we were finished," said Matthew's father, "but Charlie managed to shut her down before we went over. He banged up his knee so hard he couldn't walk."

Charlie continued. "We sat there waiting and freezing for two days until the first storm passed, and not a peep from our radio. We were out of food. So your dad took the map and compass and started out, trying to walk to Frobisher. Some say you should never leave a downed plane, but we were nearly hidden by the cliff and I guess your dad just couldn't sit there and watch old Charlie freeze to death because he couldn't walk.

"I was terrified, I tell you, when I saw your dad take out by himself. All the stories I could tell myself about the awful heat at Borroloola couldn't keep me warm. I lost all track of time."

Matthew's father spoke slowly. "When the second blizzard hit me, I thought that I was done for, but I kept on walking, traveling by the compass. Somehow," he said and shuddered, "somehow I made it through the mountains and that storm. Two days later I came down to the shore, but I was afraid of the moving ice. I was weak from hunger and parts of my face had lost all feeling. I knew I didn't have the strength to make it all the way around the bay.

"I sat down on the snow and I thought of you, Matthew, and wondered how you were, and I wished that we were together. I decided then and there that if I got back alive, I would take some kind of a steady job; go back to teaching and settle down awhile, the way you've always hoped we would. I wondered if I would ever see you again. I started feeling warm in that icy wind. It was a bad sign. Then, far away, I heard a sound like a mosquito's buzzing, and before I knew it, up came Kayak's cousin Namoni on a battered blue Ski-doo.

"He lifted me up and tied me on the seat. He had to use force to straighten out my legs. I could see him do it, but I couldn't feel a thing. I don't remember much after that until I woke up here three nights ago, feeling weaker than a kitten.

"After the big Air Force Search and Rescue plane spotted Charlie's broken chopper, the Mounted Police flew out with spare rotor blades, and that tough old outback bird, Charlie, brought Matilda in himself."

"Your dad is a strong man," said the nurse. "He must have walked almost a hundred freezing miles to find his way back here. He saved Charlie's life as well as his own. His feet are not too badly frozen and those black frost marks on his face will go away."

"What matters most," said Matthew's father, "is that we are all of us back here safe together." He paused, then shook his head. "I wanted to find copper so much I almost caused all of us to lose our lives. Well, that copper deposit is just not there . . . I guess.

"Like lots of my ideas, it didn't work. But I've still got a little bit of luck. Look, Matt," his father said, holding out a letter. "The government of the Northwest Territories has asked me to be the science teacher here. That means that as soon as the snow is gone, I can start my outdoor classes again, teaching geology in a tent right here on Baffin Island."

Matthew was quiet for a minute while he took in what his father was saying. That meant he could stay too—and be near Kayak. And he would study geology. Their secret could wait.

"That's wonderful Dad!" he finally said.

"You can teach me too!" said Kayak. "And I'll teach Mattoosie to speak Eskimo while I learn to hunt for *saviksak*—that means iron, material for making knives. You'll see I'm good at hunting." Kayak gave Matthew a knowing look and Matthew nodded slightly and grinned.

"It all sounds great to me." Charlie laughed. "The government says they will pay for thirty hours flying time while we take your students out and teach them mineral hunting from the air. We'll all be flying again together."

He paused. "Ross, just look at those two boys sitting there, smiling like a pair of koala bears. They think prospecting is easy! They think all we've got to do is fly them north in old Matilda and they'll jump out and find themselves a pile of gold!"